SUSPICIOUS HEART

When Erin discovers that her mother's home and livelihood is under threat from the disturbingly handsome Sebastian, she knows she has to fight his plans every step of the way. However, she quickly realises Sebastian is equally determined to win, and he apparently has the backing of the entire village. When a campaign of intimidation is begun against Erin and her mother, it doesn't take her long to work out that it can only be Sebastian behind it . . .

Books by Susan Udy
in the Linford Romance Library:

THE CALL OF THE PEACOCK
FORTUNE'S BRIDE
DARK FORTUNE
DANGEROUS LEGACY
REBELLIOUS HEARTS

SUSAN UDY

SUSPICIOUS
HEART

Complete and Unabridged

LINFORD
Leicester

First published in Great Britain

First Linford Edition
published 2013

A catalogue record for this book is available
from the British Library.

ISBN 978–1–4448–1723–2

Published by
F. A. Thorpe (Publishing)
Anstey, Leicestershire

Set by Words & Graphics Ltd.
Anstey, Leicestershire
Printed and bound in Great Britain by
T. J. International Ltd., Padstow, Cornwall

This book is printed on acid-free paper

1

Erin Kirkwood drove her silver grey Fiesta far too quickly down the narrow lane that led to the village of Willow Green and her mother's shop. If she hadn't been so preoccupied she would never have done such a thing.

However, on this particular day, she'd been to have a look at the plans for the new leisure centre that would ensure the destruction of her childhood home, Willow Cottage, which contained the aforesaid shop, the means of her mother's livelihood, and to say she was upset would be an understatement.

'That wretched Sebastian Rivers,' she muttered to herself, heedlessly rounding a particularly sharp bend in the road without curbing her speed one iota. 'How can he want to ruin everything to build a monstrosity like — ? Oh no!'

She slammed her foot on to the

brake, practically standing the car on end in her desperate attempt to stop, in the hope of missing the man and horse that had unexpectedly materialised in front of her.

The wretched Sebastian Rivers himself.

She could only watch, horror struck, when, as startled by her appearance as she'd been by his, the horse reared, causing the man on his back to slide off and fall heavily on to the ground. Erin didn't hesitate. She slung the car door open and leapt out, to run to the figure lying ominously still with his eyes closed.

'Oh, no. I've killed him,' she muttered. 'I don't believe it — '

So convinced was she that he was dead that she almost jumped out of her skin when he spoke.

'It's OK. Life hasn't been quite extinguished. It was a near thing though.' He struggled to sit up, his face bleached of all colour. He opened his eyes and looked straight at her. 'Oh, it's you.' He closed his eyes again as if in excruciating pain — which, for all she knew, he was. 'Good grief, woman!' he ground out. 'I know we're on opposing sides but did you have to go to such extreme lengths to win the battle?'

It was Erin's turn now to close her eyes. Not for reasons of pain, but in order to allow the events of the past few days to flash more clearly before her.

Of all the men she could have knocked off a horse, it had to be this one, she mutely groaned.

She hadn't been able to believe it when her mother had rung her. 'They're going to demolish my shop — my home — ' Jill Kirkwood had wailed. 'And no-one cares. You've got to come back, Erin. I need your support. I don't know what to do. Will your boss let you have some time off?'

'Hang on, Mum.' Erin's head was reeling. 'Who's going to demolish the shop? This is the first I've heard of it.'

'Yes, well, I didn't want to worry you unnecessarily. I thought it all might die a death; just go away. But it's not going to — '

'Mum,' Erin repeated, more firmly now. 'Explain. I have no idea what you're talking about.'

So her mother had — at some length.

A wealthy property developer called Sebastian Rivers was proposing to buy up to forty acres of Harry Stubbs' land, Harry Stubbs being the farmer who owned the land upon which the flat and shop that Erin's mother occupied stood. The building was one of a row of three cottages; he owned them all. The other tenants had already agreed to go — subject to planning permission being granted, of course.

They'd been offered alternative accommodation as well as compensation — as Jill had been. The problem was she didn't want to accept. She loved Willow Cottage with all her heart, had spent almost all of her married life there, brought Erin up in it. It was so full of precious memories that she was loath to let it go. The main memory was of her beloved husband, who had died ten years ago of a heart attack.

Sebastian Rivers planned to build a leisure centre, comprising a swimming pool, a nine hole golf course, tennis courts, a gymnasium — it would have saunas, sun beds, a high class restaurant, numerous bars and cafes, even a shop or two, it seemed. In fact, every amenity you could think of was going to be there. He was even planning to incorporate a luxury hotel. All of which meant, of course, he would have to demolish the three houses that currently stood in it its way. A small wood, home to a variety of wildlife, was also endangered.

'B-but can they do that?' Erin stuttered.

'If they secure the planning permission — and they seem set to if the rumours are correct. People want the development. They see jobs and money coming into the area — '

'OK. I'll see if I can get some time off — just a week or so. I've got some holidays due. It's short notice but I'm sure it'll be OK.'

Her employer, Hal Priestley, the MD of a moderately sized engineering business, had been very understanding, considering she was his PA and vital to his running of the business — his words, not hers — and had agreed to her having the time off.

'Just don't stay away too long,' he'd grinned ruefully. 'I can't do without you — '

Which was how, within a couple of days of her mother's phone call, she'd arrived home and was quickly installed in her old bedroom, feeling as if she'd never been away. The room was just the same. Rose printed wallpaper, cream curtains and duvet. Pink carpet on the floor. A girl's room. Even her old teddy bear was still balanced on the window-sill, and her doll's house still stood in the corner.

It had been the day after her arrival, while she'd been walking through the village on her way to meet her friend,

Sophie, that she'd caught her first glimpse of Sebastian Rivers. He'd been standing, talking to Harry Stubbs. She didn't know how, but she just knew it was him. Furious beyond measure at what she viewed as their callous disregard for her mother's happiness and welfare, she'd strode across to the pair and launched an immediate attack. Her target was the man behind it all, Sebastian Rivers.

'Are you the man who is set upon forcing a harmless old woman from her home?'

Maddeningly, Harry had laughed, slapping his thigh and saying, 'I don't think your mother would take too kindly to being described as an old woman, Erin. Harmless or not.'

Erin was too incensed to reply to that, so she ignored him and instead concentrated upon Sebastian Rivers, her eyes glaring from beneath a sweep of blonde hair, her usually full lips tightly compressed, her expression one of thunderous accusation.

'Do I take it that you're Erin Kirkwood?' Sebastian Rivers' voice was as smooth as silk. He seemed in no way put out by Erin's blunt words.

Erin nodded, pointedly snubbing the well cared for hand that was being held out to her. Even so, she couldn't ignore the amusement in the slaty eyes. So he thought it funny, did he? She'd soon change that —

'I'm not trying to force anyone — ' His jaw had firmed and a small muscle had begun to twitch.

'Oh, really!' Erin snorted. 'What would you call it then?'

'Erin,' Harry Stubbs sighed, 'your mother won't be homeless. I'm offering her another house in the village, with planning permission to convert part of it into a shop — just like the one she has now.'

Erin did turn her gaze upon him then. 'Yes, at ten times her present rent — '

'Well, the rent has been ridiculously low now for some years — '

'Before he died, my father offered to buy the house. You refused to sell it.'

'It didn't fit in with my plans then — '

'But clearly it does now.' Her tone was one of utter contempt.

'They could have bought something else. There were places on the market at the time — '

'Yes, but with no chance of securing planning permission for a shop. Anyway, my mother didn't want to move. That was her home, where she earned her living — '

'Oh, come on. Your father was an accountant. She didn't need to earn a living — '

'That's not the point. She didn't want to move — '

'Well, that was her choice. I kept the rent low because of her being made a widow. I was trying to help — .' He shrugged. 'But the truth is — we all have to make a living and that's why I'm looking to sell — '

'A living!' She snorted. 'A fortune

don't you mean? With the sale of all this land — ' She swept an arm wide to encompass the acres of surrounding land.

'Look, we farmers have to diversify. It's the way of things now, and think of how many people the leisure centre will bring in. All possible new customers for your mum — wherever she is living.'

'You can't force her out. There's the tenancy agreement — '

And that was how she'd first met Sebastian Rivers. Although to be fair, he hadn't said much. Hadn't had the chance, she now reflected, with her and Harry spitting nails at each other. Although, she had been acutely aware of his gaze throughout. In fact, if asked, she would have said it hadn't left her once.

She opened her eyes, hoping that this had all been some sort of nightmare. It wasn't. He was still there, lying flat now, eyes shut tight, his face the exact colour of putty. 'Oh no!' she whispered. He looked seriously hurt. 'Mr — ' she began tentatively.

His eyes snapped open. 'If you would be so good as to help me up, I will try,' the word was sarcastically emphasised, 'to mount my horse and move out of your way. You're clearly in a hurry.'

Erin silently groaned. He was furious. And holding her totally responsible for the unfortunate chain of events. She held out both hands, the better to hoist him to his feet. He was a tall man, six feet one or two, she'd estimate, and powerfully built. He wouldn't be a light weight.

'Do you make a habit of charging round, attacking anyone that you happen to disagree with?'

There was that glint of amusement again. The same one she'd glimpsed upon their first encounter. She wouldn't mind betting he wasn't hurt at all. He was toying with her. She withdrew her hand and straightened up.

'Please — ' he kept his hand out ' — if you'd just help me.'

Well, maybe he was hurt. Erin

11

relented. The expression of pain that crossed his face looked genuine and she didn't have it in her to ignore the plea of a possibly injured individual, so she caught his one hand in both of hers. It was smooth to the touch and warm, disturbingly so.

She pulled him to his feet. He groaned. Guilt — anxiety — resurfaced, ensuring that her words were sharper than she had intended. 'What on earth were you doing there — on a horse? I mean, this lane is so narrow — and extremely twisty — '

He was in the process of brushing himself off but he stopped at this unmistakable criticism. His one eyebrow shot up. 'Oh, such sympathy; such repentance. Do you know — ' he turned his head and made a big show of looking around, 'I didn't see a sign forbidding horse riding in this lane.' He stared at her. 'Maybe you'd be so good as to point it out.'

Erin felt herself reddening. She chewed at her bottom lip. It was the bane of her life, having skin so fair it showed every change of colour, every change of emotion. 'We-ell, actually, — um, I mean — there isn't one — '

'Precisely.' Silence descended, a silence punctuated only by the soft snorting of the horse. 'I was on my way into that field,' he indicated the barred gate behind him. 'I find riding over it is much the best way of inspecting a large expanse of land. But I'm sorry if you feel that's wrong — '

The other eyebrow lifted now. Erin felt extremely silly. Stiffly, she said, 'You must, of course, do as you wish.'

'Oh, I fully intend to. Saracen.' He swung and called his horse, who'd been contentedly grazing on the grass verge. 'Come.'

The animal obediently trotted over. Sebastian took hold of the reins and swiftly hoisted himself into the saddle — unassisted. Which only confirmed Erin's suspicion that he hadn't been hurt anywhere near as badly as he'd chosen to make out. He looked down at

Erin from his lofty position. She smiled weakly.

'Good to see you're unhurt,' she muttered.

He didn't respond, other than to subject her to an extremely penetrating gaze. She swung, intending to head back to her car.

He called after her, however. 'Ms Kirkwood, I'm sure we can reach some sort of amicable agreement over your mother's home — '

She didn't turn, she simply glanced at him over her shoulder. 'Are you? I wish I could share your confidence, Mr Rivers.'

2

The following evening, Erin went once more to visit her friend, Sophie. 'That man needs taking down a peg or two,' she ranted. She'd always been able to let off steam to Sophie, knowing that her words would go no further than the two of them. They'd been friends from schooldays, and, although they lived many miles apart these days, they'd made sure they'd kept in frequent touch by phone.

'What man?' Sophie absently asked, as she folded the last garment in the pile of ironing she'd been doing when Erin had burst in. 'Right,' she sighed, 'now that's finished — coffee or tea?'

'Wine,' Erin riposted. 'If you've got any, that is? And I'm talking about Sebastian Rivers — '

'Oh, that man. I should have guessed. He seems to be engaging your every waking thought at the moment.'

'Well, wouldn't he be yours if your mother was in the process of being evicted?'

'She's not being evicted, Erin — ' Sophie pulled a bottle of Chablis from the wine rack in the corner of the kitchen. 'This do?' She waved the bottle at Erin. 'Good job Dad brought home a few bottles last night. He must have known you'd be calling,' and she winked at her friend.

Sophie, although the same age as Erin, twenty-four, still lived with her parents, this despite having a good job as a doctor's receptionist in nearby Kinnerton. In fact she was dating said doctor's son, Hector, who had followed in his father's footsteps and was now sharing the practice.

'Well, what would you call it? He wants her out. The beast — '

'So, have you met him again then?' Sophie sought to hastily change the subject away from Erin's mother. Mainly because her friend looked in imminent danger of blowing a gasket. Erin, of course, had been quick to relate every detail of her and Sebastian's first encounter.

'Well, not met — exactly.' Erin's heartbeat quickened as she recalled the exact circumstances of the encounter. She could have killed him, for heaven's sake.

'What do you mean?'

'I knocked him off his horse — yesterday — while I was driving along the lane.'

'You what?' Sophie squeaked. 'That's something — even for you. Tell me,' she eyed her friend, 'was it deliberate or not?'

'Of course it wasn't deliberate.' Erin was indignant. It was bad enough that Sebastian Rivers had intimated that.

For Sophie to think she was capable of doing such a thing?

Sophie snorted, 'Humph, I wouldn't put it past you.'

'Sophie! What sort of person do you think I am?'

'Well — despatching Sebastian Rivers from the face of the earth would be one way of solving your problem.' Mischievous amusement glinted at Erin, belying the seriousness of her words. 'Might have the villagers up in arms, mind you. They — to a man and woman — they all want the leisure centre.' There was a disturbingly calculating expression upon Sophie's face now, banishing all trace of the humour of just seconds ago.

'As we very well know, it was an accident. But — ' it was Erin's turn now to eye her friend, 'what about you, Sophie? Are you with us or against us?' The question wasn't quite as light-hearted as it sounded.

It was important to Erin that her closest friend supported her in her fight. If she couldn't rely on Sophie, who could she rely on?

But Sophie wasn't about to confirm either her support or her opposition. 'Oh, somewhere in the middle.'

'I see. Maybe you'd better explain that.'

'Gladly. I can see the benefits to the community as well as the drawbacks. I mean, I sympathise with your mum, but I have to say it would be good to have the centre. It would instil some much needed life into this village.'

'Hmmm.' Erin sipped thoughtfully at her wine, taking one of the crisps that Sophie had just put down in front of her.

'Given up on the diet then?'

Erin defiantly popped it into her mouth. 'Just one won't hurt.' She waged a constant battle to keep her figure under control — especially when anyone placed either crisps or chocolates in front of her.

'So,' Erin said, 'you think Mum should give up, leave her home of nineteen years and just go?'

'I didn't say that — not exactly.'

'Then what are you saying?'

'That I can see both sides.'

'I mean, why can't they leave the houses where they are and just develop the land?'

'Because the houses are right where

the entrance and car park will be. It's all part of the plan, an essential part, apparently. And anyway, would your mum want to live with all that right behind her?'

A wrinkle of doubt pulled at Erin's brow. 'I suppose not. But I really can't understand the reason for building it here — in Willow Green — when, surely, Kinnerton, as a bigger town with a much bigger population, would be a much better proposition.'

'Not really. Loads of people already pass through the village on their way to the medieval castle and Roman remains. Kinnerton isn't on that route. It will mean that Willow Green gets more visitors and they might stay for a while. It means more jobs, more money spent — some of it probably in your mum's shop. Anyway, changing the subject, what did you think of Sebastian Rivers? Tasty, huh?'

Erin shrugged. 'If you like tall, dark, sardonic-looking, arrogant men, I suppose he could be described that way.'

Sophie eyed her for a long moment and then asked, 'How's Ben?'

Ben was Erin's current man — current, that is, as far as Sophie was concerned. As far as Erin was concerned, he was about to be her ex.

'He's fine.'

'What does he feel about you hotfooting it back here?'

'I haven't asked him.' Erin spoke without thinking. She hadn't meant to tell anyone that she was about to end the relationship until she'd told Ben herself.

'You haven't — ? Oh, don't tell me. He's had the order of the boot, too?'

'He's been getting too demanding.'

'Good grief, what is wrong with you? Ever since Danny — '

Erin didn't speak. That still hurt. Too much to lightly discuss, even with her best friend.

'All good looking men are not like Danny, you know, love,' Sophie went on gently.

'Aren't they?'

'No. Just because he was unfaithful with Amanda — '

'My friend, Amanda, you mean.'

'That's why you're so hostile to Sebastian Rivers.'

'What on earth are you on about now?'

'He's good looking, breathtakingly so. The local girls are practically tying themselves in knots to get him to notice them. That's why you're so anti him, isn't it? It's not just the new centre.'

'Don't be ridiculous. If he were as ugly as sin, I would still be anti him — as you put it. Sophie, he's trying, him and Harry Stubbs, let's not forget Harry, to evict my mother. I suppose now you'll say that it's Harry's looks that are influencing me too?'

'No, but you do go for the safe bet. Opting for men like Ben Nash, in fact.'

'What's wrong with men like Ben Nash?'

'He's so — ' Sophie wrinkled her nose, 'ordinary.'

'You mean boring?'

'We-ell, if the cap fits and you'd know that better than me.'

'Soph,' Erin was growing irritated, 'the truth is, I'm just not ready to settle down and Ben is.'

'You were ready to settle down with Danny — '

'Yeah, and look where that got me. Dumped for one of my friends.'

3

It was after that that it all began. That night, while Erin and Jill slept, someone crept through the village and plastered graffiti all over the shop window. GET OUT was the main message, as well as WE WANT THE LEISURE CENTRE.

A call to the police station at nearby Kinnerton evoked little or no interest, the implication being they were far too busy to bother with such trivia, although that wasn't actually put into words.

All that was left for Erin and Jill to do was remove the garish paint.

'Who could have done this?' Jill repeatedly asked. 'What are we going to do?' She sounded defeated already. 'We can't fight every man and woman in the village.'

Erin went and put her arms around the older woman. 'Yes, we can.' She carefully kept her tone light. She didn't want her mother to guess that she was every bit as concerned. But if someone — someone from the village, Erin assumed — was prepared to do this, how much further would they go to force Jill from her home?

They'd not quite finished cleaning the window when a familiar voice hailed Erin from behind.

'Hey! I heard you'd had a visit from some local artists.'

It was Declan, Harry Stubbs' son. When they were eighteen, for six months he and Erin had been practically inseparable. It hadn't been until Declan began to talk about getting married that Erin had decided things were getting too serious and it was time to spread her wings. She'd enrolled upon a secretarial course at the college at Kinnerton and twelve months later had applied for and got the job at HP Engineering in Birmingham.

She'd commuted daily from the village for a time, but upon being promoted to the position of Hal's PA twelve months ago, had felt affluent enough to take out a mortgage on a small flat ten minutes from the factory.

She suspected that Declan still carried a torch for her and his expression now as he regarded her did nothing to lessen that suspicion.

'I was going to offer to clean it off for you,' he now declared, 'but I can see you've beaten me to it.' He strode across to Erin and put an arm around her, pulling her close enough to plant a kiss upon her cheek.

'Hello, Declan.' Without making too much of a business of it, she freed herself.

'Look, I wanted to say, all this leisure centre business, it's nothing to do with me. It's all down to Dad.'

'Oh, I see.'

'I wouldn't want it to come between you and me, Erin.'

'There's no reason why it should.'

'In that case, how about joining me for a drink tonight?'

Erin was acutely aware of her mother's encouraging glance. She knew instantly what Jill was thinking. That if Erin and Declan grew close once more, maybe Erin could persuade Declan to use his influence on his father to try and stop the development. But, much as Erin loved her mother, she wasn't prepared to embark upon a love affair purely to influence the Stubbs men.

'We-ell, I don't know.'

'Oh, come on. It's just a drink between old friends. Nothing more.' Declan's smile was immensely engaging, reminding her of the days when he could switch on the charm like a light bulb.

So she didn't really need Jill urging, 'Yes, go on, darling,' to make her accept. And when all was said and done, she'd be extremely reluctant to lose Declan as a friend.

'All right. Where and what time?'

'Ms Kirkwood. Mrs Kirkwood. I want you both to know how much I regret what's happened.'

Both Jill and Erin swung to find themselves staring directly into Sebastian Rivers' good looking face. And suddenly, Declan seemed overshadowed, diminished — much to Erin's annoyance.

Erin had told her mother what had happened, naturally, and she watched now as Jill's keen eyed gaze searched for any signs of injury in Sebastian.

'Oh, it's you,' was Erin's low keyed response.

'Yes, it's me.' After a single glance at Erin, he turned to address himself to Jill, holding out a hand as he did so. 'We haven't actually met yet. I'm Sebastian Rivers.'

'Yes, I know,' Jill responded, flashing him a warm smile and taking his hand. 'I do hope you're not any the worse for your fall. Erin told me.'

Erin could only glare at the back of her mother's head, not quite believing what she was hearing. This wretched man was their sworn enemy and here was her mother politely enquiring after his health.

'Some bruises, but nothing that won't heal. Which is somewhat surprising, given that your daughter is nothing if not thorough.'

He continued to ignore Erin, much to her fury. 'It was an accident,' she muttered. 'But sorry.'

'Such graciousness,' he murmured, turning his head just far enough to cast a cool glance at her.

However, as he almost at once looked back at Jill again, Erin decided she may as well be invisible for all the heed he was paying her. And that irritated her more than anything else.

'I'm truly sorry,' he went on, 'about all of this.'

He indicated the remains of the graffiti still showing on the shop window. And Erin had to admit that he did look concerned — which was strange, considering that he was the one who wanted Jill out — just as the words had said.

For the first time then, Erin wondered if he could be behind it? And not one of the villagers as she had initially presumed.

Oh, not him personally — she couldn't imagine Sebastian Rivers sneaking along in the dead of night to spray paint someone's window, but maybe he'd paid someone else to do it?

'Have you informed the police?'

'Yes,' put in Erin bluntly, 'and suffice it to say, it didn't feature very highly on their list of priorities.'

It was now that Declan must have decided he'd been ignored for long enough because he said, 'I hope the graffiti wasn't down to you, Rivers.'

Erin could have kissed Declan for putting her own thoughts so succinctly into words.

As for Sebastian, he looked as if he'd been struck. His face paled and his eyes, already the colour of a storm cloud, darkened even further.

'Do you really see me sneaking along and spraying paint over someone's shop window, Stubbs?' His top lip curled contemptuously at the other man. 'It's more likely to be one of the villagers, don't you think? They all want the development, as I'm sure you know.'

Declan didn't answer so Erin did it for him. 'It was a reasonable enough question, in my opinion.'

'Oh, really? As reasonably as you knocking me off my horse, presumably.'

Erin heard Declan gasp, 'You didn't?'

She nodded. However, Sebastian seemed oblivious to this and, once again ignoring Erin and Declan, said to Jill, 'It's been good to meet you, Mrs Kirkwood. Please accept my assurance that the graffiti was not of my doing. Not my style at all. Good day.' And he strode off, his back noticeably stiff with anger.

'Well,' Declan exclaimed, 'that touched a sore spot.'

'Declan, don't ever do such a thing again,' Jill remonstrated. 'I am perfectly capable of fighting my own battles.'

Which was a bit rich, Erin mused, coming from the woman who'd rung her, tearfully pleading for her to come and support her.

*   *   *

As she'd promised, that evening Erin went to meet Declan at the Red Lion, the only pub that the village possessed and the pub wherein Declan worked part-time. It was his evening off.

Once they were seated at a table for two Declan once again raised the subject of Sebastian Rivers.

'You don't want to take any notice of Rivers' weasel words, you know, Erin. I wouldn't trust him as far as I could push him. That graffiti, it was just the sort of thing he'd pay someone to do, enabling him to declare — quite legitimately — that he hadn't done it.'

Once again, Declan was echoing Erin's own thoughts. They did seem to be coming from the same place. Unexpectedly, she felt closer to him than she'd done for years.

'Yes, I had the very same notion.' She stretched out a hand to him, which he wasted no time in taking hold of.

'Oh, you can count on me,' he

confirmed, squeezing her fingers tightly before lifting them to plant a kiss upon them. 'You know, I've never quite got over you, Erin.'

'So this is why you ended things with me, you — you rat, you! So you could sit and canoodle with her!'

Erin gasped. Canoodle? She looked up into the blazing eyes of Laura Kilgrew, Declan's girlfriend of twelve months. Good grief, where was this woman coming from? It would be funny if it wasn't so embarrassing.

She tried to pull her hand free of Declan's grasp, not wishing to inflame the situation any more than was necessary, but he refused to let go. Making his last stand? Erin wondered.

'I knew you still had feelings for her. No matter how often you denied it.'

'Please, Laura,' Erin began. 'You've got this all wrong.' She'd known Laura almost as long as she'd known Sophie. 'We're just having a drink.'

'Don't talk to me, you trollop. Swanning back here, just expecting to pick up where you left off. Did he tell you he finished with me the instant he knew you were here?' A sob obliterated the anguished words.

Erin's tender heart ached for the girl.

'Laura, it's not what you think. Please believe that. Declan and I are old friends, that's all. We were discussing the new leisure centre.'

'And that's another thing.' Laura glowered down at her. 'Have you stopped to consider how badly this village needs something like that? No, you're selfish.'

Contempt now replaced angry distress. 'You and your mother make me sick. She could easily move, have another shop open in a matter of weeks, but will she? No. You're selfish, both of you. And as for you, Declan Stubbs.' She swept her furious gaze back to Declan, a scarlet-faced Declan by this time, and one who was beginning to noticeably feel under the ferocity of this attack, 'you're welcome to her. In fact, you deserve each other. What I ever saw in you . . . '

By this time, the entire pub had

fallen silent, everyone staring as Laura raised her hand and struck Declan across the face. She'd just turned, clearly intending to mete out the same treatment to Erin, when she was stopped by a razor sharp voice saying, 'I wouldn't do that if I were you.'

Everyone swung to look at the person who'd just walked in.

Erin groaned.

Sebastian Rivers. Of all the people who could have come upon her in such an humiliating position, it had to be him.

4

Laura wheeled to face Sebastian. 'What's it to do with you? Just because you're trying to buy your way into this village, it doesn't give you the right to interfere.' She spat the words at him.

'I'm not interfering on that basis,' Sebastian smoothly countered her accusation, 'I'm simply not prepared to stand by and watch one person verbally and physically abuse another. Not if I can prevent it.'

'Well, butt out,' Laura shouted, oblivious to the muted gasps and giggles that were now rippling round the pub.

Erin could only sit and wait for whatever was about to happen. Although, she couldn't help wondering why Sebastian Rivers of all people should have sprung to her defence? After knocking him off his horse the way she had, and then virtually blaming him for simply being there, she'd have thought he'd stand by and applaud her attacker.

'Look,' she stumbled to her feet, 'it's OK. I can look after myself.'

'Oh, really,' Sebastian murmured, 'that wasn't how it looked to me.'

'Laura,' Erin went on, 'it's not what you're thinking.'

'Yes, it is. He's besotted with you. He always has been. It's been Erin this and Erin that.'

'Declan — ' Erin appealed to the man still sitting down, mutely pleading with him to contradict Laura's statement. But he just shrugged his shoulders and took a mouthful of his beer. In fact, now that he'd got over his initial shock, he seemed quite unconcerned about the whole thing.

Laura, too, stared at him, before, in an act of unadulterated fury, she snatched up his glass and upended it over his head.

The entire pub erupted. 'Atta girl,' they cheered.

However, their spirited encouragement

failed completely to comfort Laura. She gave a heartbroken sob and ran from the room.

Erin made to go after her. She felt terrible. As if the whole thing were in some way her fault. But Sebastian put out a hand and halted her.

'I wouldn't. She needs time and space.' He glanced down at Declan then, who was sitting, the beer literally dripping off him. 'I think you deserved that, my friend. It sounds as if you've treated her very badly.'

'Oh, mind your own business, Rivers,' Declan snapped.

'Gladly,' Sebastian bit back. He turned to Erin. 'If you're all right now?'

'I am,' was Erin's grim response. She couldn't bring herself to thank him, as ungracious as she felt. After all, she hadn't asked him to intervene.

'Then I'll rejoin my friend.' And Sebastian went back to where another man was standing just inside the room, a broad grin plastered to his face. He put a hand on Sebastian's shoulder, and murmured something. Sebastian looked back at Erin before he too said something, and then they walked together to a table on the far side of the bar.

'Humph, probably pointing me out as the troublemaker who's putting the spoke in his wheel,' she muttered.

'The other chap's his business associate,' Declan told her. 'He's responsible for putting together the finances for all of Rivers' developments.'

'Oh, I see.' Erin shot a curious glance across at the two men, who were sitting now, heads together, clearly discussing something over their drinks. 'They're obviously plotting their next move.'

'Richard Greaves is his name.'

'Have you met him?'

'Yeah. He's been to the farm a couple of times with Rivers. Smarmy devil.'

'I see.' Erin wondered if he could be the one behind the graffiti? It seemed possible if Declan was describing him as smarmy. Although to be fair, he didn't look smarmy. He glanced up at that point and caught her staring.

A small smile crossed his face. She lowered her gaze, embarrassed at being caught. He wasn't as good looking as Sebastian but he was extremely presentable, even so. With thick blond hair, he had the bluest eyes that Erin had ever seen.

She'd put him in the same age bracket as Sebastian, that was thirty-five if Jill was to be believed. He must have said something to Sebastian about her because the next thing she knew Sebastian was looking back at her too. If she could have crawled under the table at that moment she would have — gladly.

'Do you want another drink?' Declan asked.

Glad of something to distract her from the suspicion that the two men were discussing her, she said, 'It's my turn.' The last thing she wanted was for Sebastian Rivers to think she was interested in him. Or his sidekick, for that matter.

'Another beer? It's the least I can do as it was my fault in a way that your last one was poured over your head.'

Although she spoke lightly, her heart ached for Laura's anguish. She hated hurting anyone and would go to quite extraordinary lengths not to. She'd been caught quite unawares this time, not having considered even for a second how Laura would feel at spotting Erin and Declan together. Of course, what she hadn't realised was that Declan had ended things with Laura the minute he knew Erin was back.

'Well, not really,' Declan argued. 'You didn't ask me to finish with her.'

'Quite. I also didn't know you had. You could have said something.' Erin's response was a terse one. Although she didn't say so, she also hadn't asked to be dragged into their row, but she had been. She did feel it had been a little unreasonable of Laura to blame her for the demise of the relationship. It had been nothing to do with her. And Declan was a grown man, after all, perfectly able to make his own decisions about whom he wished to see.

'Are you sure you've done the right thing, though? I would have thought you and Laura were made for each other.'

He eyed her reflectively. 'The problem is — I think I'm in love with someone else.' ✓

Erin couldn't mistake his meaning, yet he didn't look at her as a man in love would. But that was Declan. Although he'd said he wanted to marry her six years ago, and seemed to be still carrying some sort of torch for her, he'd never played the role of seriously love struck suitor.

That had been one of the reasons she'd decided to leave the village. She'd reasoned that once she was out of the way, he'd quickly get over her and find someone else.

She'd always vowed she wouldn't marry anyone that she wasn't head over heels in love with and she had been a long way off that with Declan. Just as she'd decided that he was with her. Looking at him now didn't alter her view about that — despite his words to the contrary.

She went to buy the drinks and it was as she was standing at the bar, trying not to look across at the two men still talking intently, that the notion crossed her mind that the creator of the graffiti could have been Laura. She wanted the leisure centre built, her words had made that very clear, and she almost certainly wanted Erin gone. Making Erin's life here unpleasant would go a long way towards achieving both aims. So, could the words GET OUT have been aimed solely at Erin?

* * *

It was a couple of days later — Erin was serving in the shop while Jill prepared supper for them both — that Harry Stubbs came to see her.

'Erin,' was his initial, slightly stiff greeting. He evidently hadn't forgotten their earlier run in.

'Mr Stubbs,' Erin retaliated — just as stiffly.

'I thought we should have a chat.'

'If it's about your plans for the village nothing you can say will make me think any better of them. I'll never agree.'

'But it's not you that has to agree, is it, Erin?' His tone was cool and his normally genial expression was markedly absent. In fact, the pale blue eyes were cold to the point of glacial.

He was an attractive man for his fifty-five years, the tan he'd acquired through working outside most of the time enhancing that attractiveness. True, his face was lined but not overly, and his physique was that of a much younger man. Harry Stubbs looked after himself.

He'd always been fond of Jill but, since the premature death of his wife four years ago from breast cancer, that fondness had seemed to be on the verge of intensifying into something warmer. Erin knew that he and Jill had been out several times for a meal, Jill had been quite open about it. But Jill hadn't been interested in a romantic relationship and so things had cooled again between them.

Now, the news of Harry's proposed sale of land had well and truly scuppered any chance of friendship developing into something more — at least, on Jill's side.

'Well no, but Mum is dead set against it too. This is her home, after all.

'I understand that, but I'm not asking her to move miles away. I'm just proposing that she move along the road a little way. She'll be well compensated for her inconvenience. The neighbours have agreed.' He paused. 'The thing is, Erin, the scheme won't go ahead without your mum's agreement. Rivers won't buy with tenants still living on the land. Even if he gets permission.'

Erin shrugged.

'So . . . '

Erin waited for him to go on.

'Won't you reconsider?'

'But, as you've just pointed out, Mr Stubbs, it's not my decision.'

'I know, but you could persuade Jill. If you encouraged her to think of the benefits.'

'I don't think I could do that, Mr Stubbs. Because you see, I can't really see any benefits, not for Mum. She's adamant. She doesn't want to move. All her memories are here in this house, and I really don't think that any amount of compensation will make up for leaving them behind. Sorry.'

And that had been that. Harry Stubbs had left, looking very much like a dog with its tail between its legs. Erin had felt bad — she'd known Harry for years — but she couldn't let sympathy for his position influence her. It was her mother she had to consider. Nonetheless, she still felt bad; guilty, even.

For Declan had told her the other evening that the farm was simply not paying its way and something had to be done! 'Or we'll be bankrupt in six months.'

The next day Erin was walking their next door neighbour's dog, Sammy. The old lady, increasingly troubled with arthritis, was finding the daily exercise difficult, so Erin had volunteered to take over the task while she was at home. She met Richard Greaves.

Sebastian wasn't with him, but she recognised him instantly. Just as he recognised her.

'Hi there,' he called. 'Nice dog. Yours?'

'No, my neighbour's. I'm just helping her out.'

'It's Erin, isn't it?'

'That's right.'

'Yeah, Sebastian told me.' He grinned crookedly, engagingly. 'Some scene the other evening,' he added.

'Don't.' She grimaced. 'It was so awful, so embarrassing.'

He eyed her, his head to one side. 'So, are you and the chap you were with an item then?'

Erin was taken aback by his forthrightness. 'Why do you want to know?'

Erin waited. She was beginning to suspect that there was quite another reason for him stopping to talk.

She was right. 'Sebastian's a really decent chap, you know.'

'So decent he's trying to evict a woman who's spent the last nineteen years in the house, whose only memories of her dead husband are all there.'

'He's not trying to evict anyone. Your mother will receive very substantial compensation as well as another house, offered at a very reasonable rent still . . . '

'How much compensation?' Jill had never actually mentioned the amount and Erin hadn't thought to ask. It hadn't seemed important when set alongside the loss of her much-loved home.

But Richard Greaves now quoted a figure that had Erin blinking in astonishment. Why hadn't her mother mentioned it? Maybe, she hastily assured herself, because it wasn't about the money. It was about a person's right to stay in the home she wanted.

'Did you not know that?' he went on to ask.

'No.'

'Does it make a difference?'

'Not really. It's my mother you should be talking to, not me.'

'But you have influence over her.'

Astonishing that people should think that. First, Harry Stubbs, now Richard Greaves. Did Sebastian think the same? She decided to disabuse Richard of the notion. He could then tell Sebastian. Save him the trouble of approaching her.

'Not that much. I don't live here.'

'Aah.'

'So, you see, it's not me that will have to live in a village altered beyond recognition.'

Once again, she went to see Sophie — as she'd invariably done when troubled about anything.

She desperately needed to talk to someone not as closely connected to the problem. Maybe her friend could put a different perspective on things for her.

But all Sophie wanted to talk about was what had happened in the Red Lion. Apparently it was all over the village.

'Did you realise that Declan still felt that way about you?' she asked.

'No. In fact, Soph, I'm not sure that he does.'

'Really! So why would he end things with Laura now you're back on the scene if he didn't want a clear playing field with you?'

'I don't know and that's the truth. Maybe he just thinks he loves me. You know, me being his boyhood sweetheart and all that? Nostalgia?' She shrugged.

'Hmmm. Well, Laura clearly believes it. She's telling anyone who'll listen that the sooner you're gone back to where you came from the better. She's very bitter, so Declan must have said something to her.

'Oh dear. Bitter enough to daub the shop window with graffiti, do you think?'

'My goodness, you're not serious?' Sophie asked, aghast.

'I am. I don't think Sebastian Rivers was behind it. Um — I met his sidekick today, Richard Greaves. He seems nice.'

'Oh yes.' Sophie gave her an arch look.

'Not that nice! He tried to convince me of Sebastian Rivers' kindness.'

'Huh! He must have had his work cut out then.'

'Mmm. But actually it was Sebastian who stopped Laura from attacking me — as she seemed about to do.'

'Really.' Sophie's eyebrows arched until they were almost in her hairline. 'I didn't know that.'

'Yes.' Erin studied her glass of wine reflectively.

'Ho, ho. Do I detect a softening?'

'No — well, maybe a little. But I haven't changed my mind about the leisure centre. I mean — it's not just the houses that will have to be demolished, there's Willow Wood in the way too. All those lovely old trees. And they're home to heaven knows how much wildlife. It doesn't seem right. To just destroy it all.'

'I suppose not, but the new centre will bring much needed life and work. You're very much in a minority, Erin. You and your mum. I don't see how you can hold out.'

Erin found herself wondering the same thing the following morning when every customer that entered the shop berated her and her mother for not agreeing to move out.

'Just think what an improvement it will be for the youngsters here,' one woman told them. 'They've got nothing to do at the moment but hang around on the street. I'm worried sick that my Joel will get himself into some sort of trouble.'

Another woman was looking forward to maybe landing a job. 'There's going to be a hair and beauty salon in the hotel. Be real handy for me that will. Instead of having to travel every day to Kinnerton, then having to work for peanuts once I get there.'

And so it went on until five minutes before they were due to close for the day, when an elegantly dressed and extremely glamorous woman came in. Erin glanced at Jill and raised her eyebrows. This woman was a far cry from their usual customer. What on earth could she want from them?

They were soon to find out.

'How can I help you?' Jill asked. 'Only we're about to close.'

'I know. That's precisely why I left it till now.'

Erin experienced a stab of apprehension. Now what?

5

The woman held out a hand to Jill. 'You must be Mrs Kirkwood.' She then glanced at Erin. 'And you — Erin Kirkwood?'

'Right on both counts. How can we help you?' Jill asked.

'We haven't met.' The woman smiled graciously.

'No,' was Jill's polite rejoinder. 'You don't live in the village otherwise I'd know you.'

'No, I live in Kinnerton with my brother, Sebastian Rivers. Sort of an unpaid housekeeper.'

'I see. So, I ask again, how can we help you?' Jill's good-natured expression had changed to one of hostile anxiety. Erin moved closer to her mother, protectively, supportively.

'Well,' the smile had lost some of its graciousness in the face of the Kirkwoods' deliberate coolness. 'Obviously Sebastian has talked about your unwillingness to vacate these premises.' She glanced disparagingly round the small shop. She clearly was at a loss to understand Jill and Erin's fondness for it.

'I'm sure he has,' Jill said.

'What about hard cash?' The woman's face had hardened — as had her eyes.

'I've already been offered compensation.'

'Not enough, clearly. So how much do you want? I mean, let's be honest, that's the real reason behind your refusal to go, isn't it? Money.'

'How dare you?' Jill literally spat the words. 'Let me tell you, Ms . . . Mrs . . . '

'I've reverted to my maiden name now. It's Ms Rivers. Valerie Rivers.'

'Well, Ms Rivers, no amount of money will change my mind. I'm staying here and that's that. Your brother will have to build around me.'

Which even Erin could see was a ridiculous thing to say. The upheaval of the building work alone would drive Jill out of her mind. The peace and tranquillity of her surroundings had been what she'd most cherished throughout the years.

'You know they can't do that.'

'Well, there you are then. You have your answer. Better they find somewhere else to build their leisure centre.' Jill's voice broke as she continued, 'Because I'm not moving out.' She'd begun to tidy the sweet counter, her fingers trembling, so great was her distress.

'Mum . . . ' Erin began.

'This is ridiculous,' Valerie Rivers exclaimed. 'Look, we're all adults, reasonable people. Surely this can be resolved? Discussed sensibly?'

'I don't see how,' Jill snapped, evidently recovering her composure and banishing the incipient tears — all in one go. Erin felt a rush of admiration for her mother. Even with her daughter at her side, she'd needed immense reserves of will power to withstand all the opposition and hostility that was being demonstrated towards her.

'Look — why don't you and your daughter,' Valerie smiled benignly at Erin, 'come to dinner at the house? Sebastian will be there. I'll make sure of that.'

'No, thank you,' Jill snapped. 'I don't dine with the devil — not even with a very long spoon.'

'I see.'

Valerie Rivers must have the hide of a rhinoceros, Erin decided. She didn't seem in any way offended by Jill's outspokenness.

'Here's my card,' she said, 'with the address and phone number on. Think about it and give me a ring. As far as I can see, it's the only way out of this impasse.'

'Has your brother put you up to this?' Jill demanded to know.

'Sebastian doesn't even know I'm here.'

Once Valerie Rivers had left, Jill stood, staring at the card she'd been given, turning it over and over in her fingers. 'Would you credit her? As if we'd go to dinner with her and her wretched brother?'

'I know. It does seem a tad optimistic. And what would talking about it achieve? You've made up your mind.'

'Quite. So let's change the subject.' And Jill dropped the card into the bin.

Erin waited until her mother had gone to put their supper on to fish it out again and put it into her pocket. Quite why she did that she couldn't have said.

★ ★ ★

Over the next few days, the local residents continued to vent their anger about the two women's resistance to the plans. Until in the end even Erin began to wonder whether they were being too obstructive? Too stubborn? After all, Jill could open another shop, just yards away. Did it really make all that much difference which building she inhabited?

It wasn't just the house and shop that contained her memories, the village did too. And in any case, they were all there, in her head, the one place they'd never leave.

Erin was on the verge of putting these views to her mother when something happened to change her mind completely.

Once again, in the dead of night, someone crept along to push a load of rubbish through the shop letterbox. It was all that was needed to extinguish every one of Erin's doubts about what they were doing. This was blatant intimidation and she was darned if they were going to give in to it.

It had been Jill who had discovered it. Her shouts of 'Oh no!' had Erin running down the stairs from the flat where she'd been tidying up the breakfast things.

'I can't believe someone would do this,' she wailed. 'Who can it be? Surely not Sebastian Rivers?'

'Who knows?' Erin grimly replied. 'I

think we'd better go and have that dinner and try to discover exactly what he is capable of.'

Never one to tarry once her mind was made up, Erin wasted no time in ringing the number on Valerie Rivers' card.

'Hello, Valerie Rivers speaking.'

'Erin Kirkwood,' Erin said with no preamble of any sort. She wasn't in the mood for mealy-mouthed courtesy. The sooner this meeting was arranged the better. She was determined to make it absolutely clear that no amount of pressure — intimidation — would change Jill's mind.

Of course, she wouldn't actually accuse Sebastian Rivers, but she couldn't think who else would be behind something like this — other than Harry Stubbs.

'Aah, Ms Kirkwood.' There was the faintest pause. Erin waited for her to say that the rubbish incident was nothing to do with either her or her brother — for naturally, news of it had sped around the village with the speed of light.

'That's wonderful,' she said when Erin told her that she and Jill were prepared to accept her invitation to dinner. 'How would — ' Erin heard the rustle of paper, an appointments diary, she assumed, ' — Friday suit you? This Friday?'

'Fine. The sooner the better as far as I'm concerned.'

'Good. Eight o'clock then.'

Erin replaced the receiver only for the phone to immediately ring. It was the local paper, *The Chronicle*.

'I'd like to do an interview with you,' the voice on the other end of the phone said. 'We've heard about the battle going on over the new leisure centre and this latest development adds a whole new dimension to it. The editor's very keen that we put your side of the story.'

What else could Erin do but agree? And who knew? Maybe this would swing village opinion on to their side?

'It won't be in this week's edition obviously, but it will go out next week,' the reporter, Joe Beasly, told her.

Jill wasn't so sure when Erin told her what was going on. 'Oh, darling, I don't know. It could just make Sebastian Rivers even more determined. If it was him.' She shook her head. 'Oh, I don't know what's to think. He seems too much the gentleman.' She disregarded Erin's snort of contempt, 'But if it was him, he could resort to even worse tactics.'

'Or it could halt him in his tracks if he thinks we'll go public over every incident.'

How would it look, though? she uneasily wondered. To talk to the paper about his attacks, if he was the person behind them, and then sit and eat dinner at his table?

6

Joe Beasly quickly put her at ease. He was very friendly and, just as he'd promised, he asked for her side of things — which Erin unhesitatingly gave. He then mentioned the rubbish incident.

'Who do you think is behind this campaign of terror?'

'Well . . . ' Erin gulped, 'it's hardly a campaign of terror?' She gave a light laugh which erupted more as a hiccup, such was her uncertainty about what she was doing.

'I have to disagree. You've had graffiti plastered all over your shop window advising you to get out. Now rubbish through your letterbox. That's intimidation in my book — on a fairly hefty scale. Is Sebastian Rivers behind it, do you think? Or maybe Harry Stubbs? I've heard he's in fairly serious financial trouble and is very keen to sell the land involved.'

'Oh no, I'm sure they're not,' she hastened to assure him with far more confidence than she felt, it had to be said.

'Then who?' he pressed. 'Local people who are in favour of the development?'

'I really don't know.' And more than that she refused to say. She bitterly regretted having agreed to the interview in the first place. She prayed that no names would be mentioned. It could only make an already fraught situation even worse.

Friday evening duly arrived and Erin and Jill dressed themselves in appropriate finery — they were sure that Valerie would have pulled out all the stops. After all, look at how she'd dressed up simply to visit a village shop. Neither of them wanted to be made to feel inferior in some way. They were facing a difficult evening and would need all the confidence they could muster.

They pulled up in Erin's Fiesta to discover Harry parking his car.

'Did you know that Harry was invited?' Jill asked.

'No, but I suppose it was to be expected if this meeting is intended to try and resolve the situation. Although, quite how they think anything will be resolved any different when you've already made up your mind, I really don't know. No, we just need to know whether Sebastian Rivers is truly capable of the sort of intimidation we've already experienced — and if he is, what else we might expect to happen.'

The house, they saw as they climbed from the car, was a large, sprawling affair, situated at the end of a fairly long driveway. It couldn't be seen from the road because of a high hedgerow.

The gates, tall, wrought iron and reminding Erin of a row of hungry teeth — which seemed appropriate considering who their owner was, Erin grimly decided, had been standing open, ready for them to enter.

Erin eyed the honey-coloured brick-work and rows of windows. Perfectly manicured parkland stretched out on either side for as far as the eye could see. Wow!

The place screamed of riches far beyond anything she could ever hope to accrue. Why did he need to make even more money by the building of the leisure centre?

'Nice place he's got, hasn't he?' Harry said. 'First time I've been as well. Must be worth a bob or two.'

His words tailed off as the imposing front door opened and they all found themselves looking at Sebastian Rivers. A tight smile was the only sign of welcome.

Oh dear, thought Erin, he clearly doesn't want us here. We shouldn't have come.

'How nice,' he said, 'I couldn't believe it when Valerie told me what she'd arranged.' His darkening eyes, however, gave the lie to his opening statement.

For two pins then, Erin would have turned tail and fled. The manner in which his still dark gaze travelled over her, taking in every inch of her shining hair, her cream blouse and black silk trousers, had her practically shrinking in her shoes.

'How nice,' he repeated, clearly not meaning that either. Erin felt shabby and unattractive. Evidently trousers and a blouse, even though they were both made of silk, weren't good enough for dining with the high and mighty Sebastian Rivers.

He turned to Jill. 'How good of you to come. I wish I'd thought of it myself. Ah, Valerie, there you are. Our guests have arrived as you can see.' He stood to one side to allow Erin and Jill to enter, and touched Harry on the shoulder as he passed. Harry muttered a few low words to him, which, no matter how Erin strained to hear, she couldn't make out.

However, she didn't have to wonder for long what was said because

Sebastian exclaimed, with, outwardly at least, genuine horror.

'Oh Erin, Jill, how dreadful. I had no idea, I hadn't heard. Rubbish through your letterbox?'

Which did seem to suggest that it hadn't been him. Either that or he was an extremely good liar. Practised, in fact. Valerie, on the other hand, exhibited no surprise at all. She simply murmured, 'Dreadful what some people will stoop to. Now, please come through.'

Once they were seated with drinks in their hands, Sebastian demanded more details of the incident. 'Have you any idea who was behind it?'

Jill answered. 'We've no idea.'

'Harry,' Sebastian turned to the older man, 'would you have any idea?'

'Oh no, Harry wouldn't . . . ' Jill stopped talking abruptly and flushed a deep crimson.

Erin stared at her mother. It wasn't the first time that she'd found herself wondering how deep Jill's feelings went for Harry.

'That seems to suggest that you think I would,' Sebastian curtly said.

'Oh no-no,' Jill stammered, 'I'm sure, I didn't mean ... ' she limped miserably into silence, glancing appealingly at Erin as she did so.

'Erin?' He swept his slaty glance over her. It chilled the blood in her veins.

When had she given him permission to address her — or her mother, come to that — by their Christian names? she wondered indignantly. She met his gaze head on. 'I have no idea what you would or wouldn't do. I barely know you.'

His eyes narrowed to slits — dangerous slits. 'Precisely.'

'But you never know.' She shrugged her shoulders, her implication graphically clear.

'What a poor opinion you must have of me.'

'No, she didn't mean that, Mr Rivers.' Jill desperately sought to retrieve the situation.

Erin sat, silent and bitterly regretting

her impulsive words. She should have kept her suspicions to herself until she had some sort of proof. There was only one thing for it.

'I'm sorry,' she said, 'This wasn't such a good idea. I think it's best if we leave,' and she stood up, preparing to go.

'Leave?' Sebastian practically spat the word out. 'Oh, no. You've come here to try and resolve the impasse that we find ourselves in. How will your leaving achieve that? Whatever else I thought of you, I didn't have you down as a coward, Erin.'

She wondered what else he had her down as in that case? A trouble maker? Huh! That went without saying. A gold digger? If he shared Valerie's implied opinion that they were holding out for more compensation then that was more than likely.

Miserably, Erin sat down again. Why on earth hadn't she kept her mouth shut? All she'd done was put Sebastian's back up.

Not surprisingly, in the wake of this

exchange and, precisely as Erin had anticipated, dinner proved a fraught affair, and, also unsurprisingly, by the end of it they were no nearer agreement on anything.

Sebastian and Harry remained adamant that they were somehow going ahead with their plans, and Jill was equally adamant that she wouldn't move out, no matter how much compensation they were prepared to offer.

To give Sebastian his due, he didn't pressure her. He merely told her to take her time in reaching a decision.

Which remark earned him a particularly sharp look from Harry. But despite this concession, conversation around the dinner table remained stiff and both Erin and Jill were glad when the evening ended.

Sadly, they left in an even more confused state than the one they'd arrived in, with Erin none the wiser about who was behind the graffiti and the rubbish incident.

Harry, she knew, was in desperate

need of the money that settling the land would bring, according to Declan that was. But then again, she supposed it could be Valerie, acting on behalf of her brother? Or acting on her own?

She obviously cared for her brother, otherwise why would she have come to see Erin and Jill? She'd want what was best for him and that was the new development. And none of these theories took Laura into account, Declan's ex-girlfriend. Or the angry locals. Honestly, it could be anyone.

She sighed. At the end of the day, they were no further forward.

Erin's sleep that night was punctuated by dreams; disturbing dreams. Of things being pushed through the letterbox, of people shouting their anger at her.

Come the next morning, she was exhausted and depressed, neither of which was helped by the sight of Ben, her ex-boyfriend, standing in the shop doorway when she opened up.

'Ben!' she cried. 'What on earth are

you doing here?'

This was all she needed.

'I wanted to see you. I miss you. And you haven't been in touch. I was hoping for at least a phone call.' He smiled ruefully.

'You could have rung me,' was her sharp rejoinder to that. The trouble was she felt guilty. He was right, she should have rung him.

'I didn't know if you'd want me to. You were — cool when we said goodbye. Offhand. I mean, didn't you think I'd mind you just going off like that, with just a phone call?'

'I was in a rush. My mother needed me.'

'Yes, you said. I've been worried about you. Look, can I come in? I feel a bit exposed just standing here.'

Erin glanced around. There were a few people out and about, none as yet heading for the shop. Oh no! Except for one, that is. Talk about bad timing. Her eyes widened and her breathing quickened. Sebastian Rivers was heading her way and looking in the mood for confrontation.

'Erin, a word, please,' he said as he got nearer. He seemed to notice Ben then for the first time. 'Sorry. Have I interrupted something?' His expression was far from repentant. 'Who's this?'

Erin stiffened. The cheek of the man. Who did he think he was? Who Ben was was absolutely none of his business.

'Ben Nash.' Ben good-naturedly held out his hand. 'And you are?'

'Sebastian Rivers.'

He shook Ben's hand and then concentrated his attention on Erin.

She didn't know why but she had this insane urge to explain exactly who Ben was. Not that Sebastian would care, she was sure. 'Ben is a friend of mine.'

'Friend?' Ben echoed, regarding her now with some dismay. 'A bit more than a friend, surely, Erin? We have been going out for three months.'

'I see. Have you come to stay?' Sebastian asked.

There was a strange look to him now.

Erin was having difficulty defining it. Whatever — he was studying Ben with interest.

'No. I'm just here for the day. I've come to see how she's getting on with this developer who's threatening to evict . . . '

'Ben.' Erin swiftly forestalled him before he could put his foot in it and make an already difficult situation worse. Although, she mused ruefully, she'd managed that herself pretty well the evening before. 'Um — this is the developer.'

'Aah.'

'What do you want?' she demanded of Sebastian. 'I thought we'd said all we had to last night.'

'Last night?' Ben exclaimed, once more with some dismay. 'Erin? What's going on?'

'Nothing, Ben.'

'Well, not quite nothing, Mr Nash,' Sebastian put in. 'Erin obviously hasn't explained. She thinks I go about putting rubbish through letterboxes; her letterbox to be precise.'

'What?' Ben was horrified.

'No, Ben,' Erin started to say, 'I didn't . . . '

'Oh, did you not?' Sebastian asked, with deceptive mildness. 'That's not the impression I received last night.'

'Erin, you can't truly believe . . . ' Ben began.

Erin was beginning to feel like a rag doll, being yanked this way and that between the two men. It was exhausting. 'No, Ben, of course I don't. Well, at least — someone did it.'

'Well, I can assure you it wasn't me,' Sebastian said. 'And neither was it Harry. Nor was it my sister, Valerie. And if you publicly repeat your accusations, or I hear that you've as much as hinted at them, I will consider taking some sort of action. Do I make myself clear, Ms Kirkwood?'

'Oh dear, what's happened to the Erin of last night?' she sarcastically asked.

Sebastian didn't answer. Instead, he

directed a bleak stare her way before swivelling on his heel and departing with a curt, 'Nice to meet you, Nash.'

'I say, Erin, whatever's got into you?' Ben asked in total astonishment. 'You can't seriously think he did such a thing?'

'I don't know what to believe if you want the truth, Ben. Anyway, come in. you're right we can't stand here.'

An hour later the job was done. She'd told Ben it was over between them.

'Is it Rivers?' he'd demanded to know.

'Wh-what do you mean?'

'Are you in love with Rivers?'

'No!'

'Are you sure? Because the chemistry between you was unmissable.'

'Good grief, of course I'm sure. He's in the process of trying to evict my mother from her home, for heaven's sake. He's the last man in the world I'd fall for.' Wasn't he?

7

If Erin thought she had problems then, within a few days everything had worsened a hundred fold.

Two dozen copies of *The Chronicle* were delivered to the shop. Erin picked one up and almost passed out, right there and then. The front page headline in large black letters was, *CAMPAIGN OF TERROR BEING WAGED ON LOCAL SHOPKEEPER*. And Joe Beasley hadn't stopped there. He'd repeated, word for word, all that Erin had said, plus a few things she hadn't said, all but accusing Sebastian Rivers and Harry Stubbs of being the perpetrators.

Should rich and powerful developers be allowed to ride roughshod over little people — all in the name of money? he asked. *This paper doesn't think so. Give us your views, folks. Stand up for the little man — or woman.*

'Oh no!' she moaned. Whatever was Sebastian going to say? What sort of action had he been considering taking?

She didn't have to wait long to find out.

Within half-an-hour, he was striding into the shop, paper in his hand, his expression one of furious outrage.

'Um, Mr Rivers,' Jill began, because of course Erin had showed her the paper straight away.

'Oh, my Lord, Erin,' she'd cried, 'now we're in trouble!'

And, my goodness, weren't they?

Erin resisted the temptation to turn and hide. Instead, she scurried behind the counter. He'd have to leap that now to get at her. Not that she didn't think he wouldn't. He looked positively murderous. And she was his intended victim. That was very evident by the way he thrust the offending newspaper at her.

'Are you responsible for this?' he demanded.

'Um — y-yes, I suppose so. But I — '

'It practically accuses me and Harry

of being behind both the graffiti and the garbage. It's almost libellous.'

'It doesn't actually accuse you,' she protested in vain.

'As good as.'

Jill had vanished, Erin noticed. Great! Even her mother had deserted her.

Then she noticed that he was striding round the counter, towards her. Her heart all but stopped. 'I-I didn't tell him it was you. He m-made th-that assumption, all on . . . all on his . . . his own.' She was gabbling now, the words tripping over each other as she hastened to make excuses. 'I explicitly asked him not to name names.'

'Well, he clearly didn't listen, did he?'

He was only inches away from her now. Erin looked beyond him, silently praying that someone — anyone — would come in. Where were all the customers? Normally they were queuing out of the door by this time. Surely someone was going to arrive and save her from this-this madman?

'If you touch me,' she stammered, 'I'll — I'll . . . '

He was so near that she could feel his breath on her face. 'Oh, I'll touch you all right.'

He paused. Marshalling his forces for the attack upon her? she wondered weakly. Which method would he use to silence her?

'You are the most exasperating woman I've ever had the misfortune to meet, Erin Kirkwood,' he went on in a low voice.

Her eyes snapped open again. He was dangerously close. She couldn't just feel his breath on her face, she could see every pore of his skin.

'I'm sorry. I don't mean to be,' was all she could lamely say. She chewed at her bottom lip. How pathetic was that?

He gave a snort of laughter. 'Don't you?'

'N-no, I just can't seem to help myself.'

'No, I can see that.'

She was fidgeting beneath the intensity of his gaze, only just stopping herself from hopping from foot to foot. 'But I do have to . . . '

But obviously he didn't want to know what she had to do, because he halted her stumbling words by the simple method of grabbing hold of both of her shoulders and pulling her forward the necessary inch to capture her mouth with his.

It had been the very last sort of action that Erin had expected. She froze, literally, enabling him to slide his arms about her, thus tightening his hold on her, as he deepened the kiss till she thought she was in imminent danger of exploding into flames. Distantly, she heard someone groaning and realised to her shame that it was her.

'Yes,' he suddenly murmured, not removing his lips from hers, 'the most exasperating, maddening woman I've ever met,' before releasing her and asking, 'You have to — what?'

Erin gasped. It was as if the kiss hadn't happened. He'd picked up the conversation exactly where they'd left it. He had some nerve, she'd give him that.

Erin felt a stab of pure rage then. Who did he think he was? One minute he was shouting at her, the next kissing her. And it seemed not to have affected him one iota.

She dashed a hand across her lips, pointedly wiping off the feel of his mouth on hers, desperately trying to halt the trembling that was threatening to remove her legs from beneath her.

'How dare you do that?' she whispered. Not only were her legs about to go from under her but she also seemed to have lost the use of her voice.

'Oh, I dare. And if you fling any more accusations around, I'll . . . ' There was an unnerving coldness to him now as he let his words trail off.

The man was inhuman, she decided. He'd all but reduced her to a heap of quivering jelly, while he . . . he stood there, icily cold but still in perfect control of himself.

'What?' she yelled, her anger finally bursting free at what he had managed to do to her. 'You'll do what?'

He didn't answer for an endless moment. Erin shuddered. What was coming now? Another kiss? She began to shake uncontrollably. Then he spoke, his voice deep and throaty.

'Erin, surely we can deal together better than this?' There was no trace of his earlier anger. It had completely vanished. Even his slate eyes had warmed. So much so, that they glinted with minute gold specks.

Well, that proved it. He was definitely inhuman. He had to be, to be able to transform himself so completely from one second to the next. He clearly didn't have a normal emotion in his body.

'I don't see how,' she grimly responded.

'Well,' a small smile flirted with the corners of his mouth, 'we just have, haven't we?'

'What?' He was confusing her again. He seemed to have an unerring ability to do that as well — again at a second's notice. She wrinkled her brow. 'What do you mean?'

'Do I really have to spell it out?'

Erin stared at him, aghast. 'If you mean what I think you mean, you're mad. Out of your mind. I wouldn't even contemplate such an idea.'

'Shame. It could work rather well.'

He looked distinctly amused. Which, of course, only fuelled Erin's fury.

'Oh, get out.' She could feel her cheeks flaming. He'd made a fool of her — again. 'Get out!'

'Erin!' It was Jill. 'I heard you shout, are you OK, darling?'

'I'm fine, Mother. And once Mr Rivers leaves, I'll be even better.'

Sebastian had indeed left them. She just wished he'd leave her thoughts as speedily, she some time later agonised. Leave her as she'd been before that kiss. For try as she might, she couldn't get it out of her head. She relived it, over and over, every single second of it, desperately trying to come up with an acceptable explanation for her heady response to it. Almost melting at one moment, and driven by heart-stopping excitement the next.

She couldn't be attracted to Sebastian Rivers; she couldn't be.

Yet Ben had sensed something between them.

Oh no. This couldn't be happening. Maybe she should return to Birmingham and her work? Get as far away from Sebastian as she could. But — would Birmingham be far enough?

Maybe Australia would be better?

As if her anxieties had transmitted themselves to him, her boss, Hal, called her the next day.

'Erin,' he said, 'how're you doing? I thought I'd ring and see if there was any chance of you coming back?'

'Oh, Hal.' Here was her excuse to leave, was all Erin could think. All perfectly legitimate. Hal needed her back. So, why did she hear herself saying, 'Not at the moment.'

'Oh heck! I can't do without you for much longer. I'm up to my ears.'

'Look, Hal, this isn't fair for you. I'll resign.'

'Erin!' he exclaimed. 'Is that necessary?'

'Well, I simply can't say when I'll be able to return. Things are a bit difficult here. I really can't leave my mother to cope alone. It means you can hire another PA.'

'But how will you manage for money and so on?'

'Oh, I'll manage. I do have some savings.'

And that was that. She was officially out of work as from now. No income, no job. She groaned. Why had she done that? Why hadn't she leapt at the opportunity to leave the village? To leave Sebastian Rivers?

She didn't know and that was the truth.

And what was she going to do? It was true, she did have some savings, but how long would they last? Then there was her flat, the mortgage payments were pretty hefty and could soon swallow up her money. She'd have to sell it, but not yet. Maybe things would work themselves out here? Maybe she'd find a job here? Or in Kinnerton? But she'd still have to sell the flat.

Her heart sank. She was so proud of that flat, at how well she'd done. But there was no way she could earn the sort of money she'd earned in Birmingham down here. The sort of money needed to pay the mortgage and live.

Was she crazy? She should be doing everything she could to dislodge the memory of Sebastian's kiss from her head. And leaving would surely have done that? So why wasn't she? She simply didn't know.

All of which meant that when Declan called into the shop to ask her out, she instantly agreed. Even with the risk of Laura going on the attack again hanging over her. Anything was better than sitting at home, moping over things. Things? She meant Sebastian, so why didn't she say so?

'There's a film I wanted to see,' Declan said. 'I thought we could go and then get some supper afterwards.'

'OK. But do you think Laura will put in an appearance again?' She couldn't help herself, she had to ask.

'I shouldn't think so.' For all his outward calm, though, Declan looked distinctly uncomfortable at that prospect.

'You wouldn't think? You're not sure then? Declan?'

'Well, she is hanging round me a bit. Can't seem to accept that it's over between us. Mind you, she wasn't this keen before. Which does make me wonder whether it's the money that Dad and I will make over the new development that's the real attraction.'

Erin stared at him. 'You seem very sure that it will all go ahead. And what do you mean? The money you and your dad will make? I thought it was nothing to do with you. It was all Harry.'

'It is — for now. But it will all come to me — eventually.' His face had reddened. 'I didn't mean now, of course.'

'I thought you were on our side?'

'I am. I am,' he insisted. 'But, you know, if it goes through, well . . . '

'I see.'

'Aw, come on, Erin. I'm just being realistic, love. I mean, even you must see that you've got an uphill battle to get it stopped. That doesn't mean I'm not on your side.

'Hey, what's wrong?'

Declan closed the gap between them and put his arms round her. 'Don't let Sebastian get to you.

'Erin, love,' he paused, 'you don't think it might be better for you and Jill, in the light of what's happened so far, to just take the compensation and move out? I mean, would it be so bad? Your mum would still have her shop in the village.'

'You mean give in?'

'Well, I suppose.'

'No, Declan. How can you suggest such a thing? It would be letting that man win, if it is him behind the vandalism. No way! Just no way! If we give in to people like him where will that leave us all? How can you think we would? I'm astonished!'

Declan lifted both hands in surrender. 'OK. No need to have a hissy fit. I just thought it might be easier all round. I mean, who knows what he'll do next? I just worry about you, you and your mum.'

They did go to the cinema that evening and, to Erin's relief, Laura didn't put in an appearance. In fact, considering the heated disagreement she and Declan had had earlier, the evening went surprisingly well.

They had a delicious supper in a small Italian restaurant afterwards where Declan seemed to put himself out to entertain her. Maybe because he'd upset her so deeply with his suggestion that she give in to Sebastian Rivers?

But despite all of Declan's attentions, Erin found she couldn't stop her thoughts straying to another man. A dark haired, dark eyed man. An exasperating man, but nonetheless a man who wouldn't seem to leave her alone.

So much was he in her thoughts that even when Declan kissed her goodnight, his sardonic features interposed themselves between them. In a desperate bid to drive Sebastian Rivers from her head, Erin returned Declan's kiss more warmly that she had ever meant to.

'Wow!' said Declan once it was over. 'Wow! The feelings haven't all gone then?'

Erin simply smiled up at him, berating herself for bestowing hope where there was none. That hadn't been fair. To use poor Declan to try and forget Sebastian. She felt ashamed. Even more so, when Declan smilingly asked, 'Any chance of us getting back to where we were before you left for Birmingham?'

'I don't know, Declan.' She bit her bottom lip. How could she cruelly dash his hopes with a blunt 'No.' after raising them in such a heedless fashion? 'Let's take things a step at a time.' She tried to ignore the extinguishing of the light within his eyes.

But the truth was she'd like nothing better than to replace all thoughts of Sebastian with Declan. Still, who knew? Maybe if she tried really, really hard, she'd be able to do just that?

★ ★ ★

'I've resigned from my job.'

Jill looked at her daughter, aghast. 'Oh, darling. Is that my fault? I should never have asked you to come back. It was selfish, look go back to Birmingham. Ring Hal now and tell him you made a mistake.'

'No. I'm not leaving while you're in danger of losing your home.' She stopped talking, belatedly noticing that her mother was dressed to the nines. 'Where are you going?'

Jill didn't seem to want to meet Erin's gaze. Instead, she looked down, fiddling nervously with the neckline of her dress. 'Out — um, with a friend.'

'You didn't say what friend?'

'Nina.'

'Nina Harcourt?'

'Yes, that's right.'

'My goodness! You're obviously going to be hitting the high spots the way you're dressed.'

And that was no exaggeration. It had been a long time since Erin had seen her mother looking so glamorous. Mind you, she supposed she wouldn't have done, not living at home any more. Still, it did seem a great deal of trouble to go to for a female friend.

'Not really. We're going for a meal at Wheelers.'

'Wow!'

Again, Jill anxiously fiddled with the dress, the bodice this time. 'Is it too much, do you think?'

8

Erin stared at her, at the tight fitting bodice. 'We-ell, it depends who else is going to be there.' Wheelers was a high class restaurant, some might even say, exclusive. Expensive, certainly. Also, at least five miles outside of Willow Green. But did people really dress this glamorously to go?

'No-one, just Nina.' A hint of red tinged Jill's cheek.

'It might be expensive,' Erin murmured. 'Can you and Nina afford it?' Jill had been widowed for over ten years now, and Nina divorced for almost that long. It was time they both met someone else. She didn't understand, if that's what she was doing, why Jill didn't just say so. Could it be that she feared Erin's disapproval?

'We've been saving up.'

'Special occasion, is it?' Maybe it was

Nina's birthday or something?

'Not really.' Jill spoke absently. She shrugged her shoulders into a fine-knit jacket. 'I must go. Nina will be waiting.'

There was the sound of a car drawing up outside.

'That will be the taxi.'

Erin continued to stare at her mother, at the flushed cheeks, not all down to the blusher she'd applied, Erin suspected, and the shining eyes. There was something going on here.

Still, it wasn't any of her business. If her mother didn't want to tell her, that was her affair. Erin snorted with silent laughter. Maybe she'd just hit the nail on the head. Her mother was having an affair. 'OK. Have a good time then.'

It was a couple of days later that Valerie Rivers made her second appearance in the shop.

'I wondered if we could go and have a coffee somewhere — Kinnerton, maybe?' Valerie asked.

'Oh, I don't know.' And Erin didn't. She wanted nothing more to do with the Rivers family. Especially not with Sebastian.

'Come on,' urged Valerie, 'I have a feeling we could become friends.'

Friends! Erin's mouth dropped open. Was the woman mad? Her brother was threatening to deprive Erin's mother of her home and build some ghastly modern leisure centre in its place. How on earth could they be friends?

Still, maybe if Erin worked on Valerie, she could persuade Sebastian to leave Jill alone? To build his leisure centre somewhere else. It was worth a try, at least.

'OK. Let me just tell my mother. She'll need to take over from me . . . '

Thus it was that fifteen minutes later, Erin and Valerie, an unlikely pair if ever there was one, were sitting in the Copper Kettle at Kinnerton, drinking cups of creamy latte and munching on a couple of Danish pastries.

'So,' Valerie invited, 'tell me about yourself. What do you do — when you're not fighting off my brother?'

Erin eyed her uncertainly. Surely Sebastian hadn't told her about their kiss? 'Fighting off?'

'Yes. Trying to halt his development.'

'Oh, yeah, right.'

'What did you think I meant?'

There was a discernible twinkle to Valerie's eye now. And again, Erin wondered what Sebastian had said to her? Surely he didn't confide to such an extent in his sister?

'Oh, nothing. Um . . . actually, I'm not doing anything at all.' She'd decided on the spur of the moment, admittedly, to be honest and up front about her situation. What harm could it do after all?

On the contrary, it would demonstrate her total commitment to stopping Sebastian Rivers in his tracks. Force him to see her as someone to be reckoned with; force him to take her seriously, more seriously than he'd done so far, maybe? 'I handed in my resignation so that I can stay here and continue the fight.'

'Bit drastic, isn't it?' Valerie took a sip of her coffee, all the while studying Erin over the brim of the cup. 'Giving up your job? I mean what will you do for money?'

'I have savings. Of course, I will also need a job.'

'Maybe I can help on that front.' Valerie was still studying Erin, her expression a strange one. Calculating, almost.

'Really!' Erin wondered what was coming now?

'Mmm. I need an assistant. Well, a secretary, actually.'

'Do you?' Erin was astonished. What on earth could Valerie need a secretary for? She didn't work, did she? Other than to keep house for her brother. Maybe she needed her recipes jotting down? Erin had to suppress a grin.

'Yes. I do a lot of charity work. I also sit upon various committees. Which means I have a great deal of correspondence to deal with. My um, typing leaves a great deal to be desired, and

I'm not terribly practical. For instance, the workings of a PC are a complete mystery. I've never managed to master one.'

Erin wasn't surprised. Whatever else this lovely woman was, she didn't look the practical sort. However, she was surprised to hear that Valerie involved herself in charitable works. She hadn't had her down as the type.

'So — what would you want me to do?'

'Well, all of my correspondence, keep my diary, make any travel arrangements necessary, things like that. I'd pay you, of course,' and she named a figure that had Erin blinking. It wasn't as much as she'd earned in her previous job but it would certainly go some way towards easing the situation in which she currently found herself. 'You can drive, presumably?'

'Yes.'

'Splendid. Because you could also act as my chauffeur. I detest driving long distances, or in cities.' She shuddered theatrically. 'All that terrifying traffic. So . . . ' she studied Erin intently, 'what do you say? You'd be doing me a great favour.'

What else could Erin say but yes. 'It would only be temporary, of course.'

'Naturally. I realise you'll want a proper job again sooner or later. Um, there's just one thing . . . ' she hesitated, 'you'll have to come to the house to work. Would that pose a problem?' Again, she hesitated. Clearly she meant because her brother would be there some of the time.

'I don't see why it should.' As long as he keeps out of my way and I keep out of his, Erin silently added. Much more to the point however, in Erin's view, was how would he feel about her working for his sister?

* * *

But if she was worried over Sebastian's feelings about her working for his sister, Jill's came as no surprise.

'You're working for that man? Erin, how could you?'

'I'm not working for Sebastian Rivers, I'm working for his sister,' Erin pointed out.

'Same thing in my book. They're both called Rivers.'

'No, it's not the same thing, Mother.'

'So, tell me how it's different.'

'Valerie doesn't have anything to do with her brother's business. I'll be helping her organise her charity work.'

'Charity work! Anyone less likely to be involved in charity work than Valerie Rivers, I can't imagine,' Jill snorted. 'She's probably hoping to get you on their side.'

'You know that will never happen,' Erin quietly contradicted. 'I need the money and she's going to pay me.'

'I told you to go back to Birmingham. Please, Erin, don't do this.'

'She's actually quite nice once you get to know her. She's nothing like her brother.'

And she wasn't. She didn't have the

arrogance that Sebastian possessed. The drive to make money at everyone else's expense, with no regard or respect for his victim's feelings. She couldn't imagine him doing anything out of charity.

But there she was wrong because, within a few hours of working with Valerie, she discovered that Sebastian also supported several charitable organisations — and not just with cash.

Valerie told her, 'Sebastian organises and pays for annual trips to the seaside for many of the deprived children. Do you know, some of them have never seen the sea before.'

Thereby making Erin feel thoroughly ashamed of her low opinion of him. 'So, if you could type some letters — I've made notes of what they need to say. You can put it all into some sort of order, can't you? And then ask Sebastian to sign them. The PC's through there and Sebastian's office is across the hallway.'

Erin only just stopped herself from groaning out loud. She'd never have agreed to do this if she'd imagined, for a second, she'd be forced to have dealings with him. She'd presumed he'd have an office somewhere else. Some grand building in central Birmingham. Not to find him working from home.

Which was how Erin found herself standing before Sebastian, holding out a sheaf of letters.

'Your sister asked me to, um, to ask you to sign these, please.' Nervously, she handed them to him, expecting an explosion at any minute at the sight of her unexpectedly appearing before him in his own home.

But Sebastian gave no indication of surprise at seeing her there, which suggested to Erin that Valerie had already warned him. He merely took the letters and walked to the desk that sat slantwise across the corner of the room, where he began to sign them without as much as a glance at what they said.

'Don't you want to check that they're all correct?' Erin asked.

He glanced up at her, his pen poised over the last of them. 'Why? I know what they all say, I told Valerie what I wanted. And I'm sure you're perfectly capable of putting together a comprehensible and grammatically correct letter.'

'Well yes, but . . .

'But what, Erin?'

His look was cool, giving no indication that he recalled, in any way, their last encounter. Erin pursed her lips in annoyance. Which just went to show, she told herself, that he probably kissed so many women that one more was neither here nor there. Why should she expect anything else? In fact, he'd probably forgotten all about it.

'Well, I've always been told you should never sign anything you haven't read,' she primly told him.

'Have you now?' He held her gaze for a long moment, the amusement that was becoming so familiar to her lightening the slate grey of his eyes. 'Well, in that case, if you think I should . . . ' before he pointedly, and with maddening thoroughness, read each and every one of the letters. It was a full five minutes before he handed them back to her, after he slowly signed the very last one.

Erin all but snatched them from him, choosing to ignore the provocative grin that tilted the corners of his mouth.

'Entirely correct,' he said, 'just as I'd anticipated.'

'Thank you,' she ground out from between clenched teeth.

'So-o,' he drawled, leaning back in his chair, to clasp his hands in front of him and subject her to intense scrutiny, 'how do you think you'll like working for Valerie . . . ' he paused, deliberately it seemed to Erin, ' . . . and me?'

That shook her. 'For you?' she echoed. 'I was under the impression that I worked for Valerie.'

'You do, but you'll also be working for me.' The slate eyes had turned stormy, his mouth tightened. Not only was she starting to recognise his amusement, she was also learning to detect the signs of his displeasure. He sighed. 'Is that a problem, Erin?'

'Um — well, Valerie said I'd be working for her, helping her organise her charitable duties.'

'You will be, but you'll also be helping me out. So? As I said, is that going to be a problem?'

'No, I s'pose not,' she muttered. Why did she feel like a schoolgirl standing, full of contrition, before a censorious headmaster?

'Sorry?' He cupped an ear. 'I didn't quite catch that.'

She glared at him. He was doing this deliberately. Openly relishing his part in making her feel small. He was all but grinning, for heaven's sake.

'No, I suppose not,' she repeated, slowly and distinctly as if she were speaking to an elderly deaf person.

Of course, that didn't pass him by. He did grin now. 'Oh dear,' he sighed again, ruefully this time, 'only suppose?'

He was mocking her.

'Only I'd heard that you'd resigned from your job.'

'You did?' Valerie must have told him.

Either that or news travelled very fast around here.

'Yes, Harry told me.'

'Harry!' How on earth did Harry know? She hadn't told him, him or Declan. Maybe he'd seen Jill and she'd told him? Yes, that must be it.

'So I suggested to Valerie that she offer you the post of secretary to both of us. Did she not make that clear?' he smoothly concluded.

'No.' In fact, Valerie had given no indication that she already knew Erin was out of work. The exact opposite, in fact, down to sounding genuinely surprised when Erin herself had told her the news.

She'd made it sound as if the job was a spur of the moment idea. Why? The answer, of course, came to her immediately. Because she knew that if Erin suspected that the offer came directly from Sebastian, she would most likely refuse it.

Which made Erin question why they should be so keen to employ her, their chief adversary? Was it a bid to gain her loyalty in the anticipation that that would weaken her opposition to their plans? Or was it because they hoped that working for them, being dependant upon them for her income, would persuade her to view their plans with more favour? Her and her mother? Persuade them, in fact, to accept the offer of compensation and move out of the cottage and shop.

Jill had certainly implied that when Erin told her what she was about to do. It seemed a more reasonable suspicion now. And she'd played right into their hands.

She was tempted, there and then, to simply terminate the agreement to work for them, but what if being here provided her with some sort of insight, or even better, inside information, about what they were planning next? It would be worth swallowing her pride and working for Sebastian simply for that opportunity. She took a deep breath. Much as she hated the idea, she'd stay.

'Aah.' He shrugged, making her acutely

aware of the breadth of his shoulders, the sheer power of him. 'Well, if you want to reconsider?'

'No.' Apart from the benefits of staying on, she really couldn't afford to turn this job down, on the basis that she didn't think she'd find another locally. Not one this well paid, at least.

'Good. Now that we understand each other, maybe you'd drive Valerie and I to Birmingham? We've a couple of meetings arranged and it would help considerably if we could study and discuss the relevant papers on the way.'

Erin half expected Sebastian to provide her with a chauffeur's uniform and demand that she wear it. When he didn't, she drew a deep breath of relief.

He and Valerie sat in the back of his pale blue BMW as Erin, somewhat cautiously it had to be said, she'd never before driven such a large and expensive car, drove them both to Birmingham. They talked in low voices all the way, occasionally studying the papers Sebastian had mentioned. Erin wondered if they concerned his planned development in Willow Green.

They reached the venue for the meeting, a luxurious five star hotel, and Erin parked the car. The pair in the back got out, Sebastian leaning forward as he did so to say, 'Go and have a coffee or something. There's an excellent cafe inside.'

'It's quite all right,' she stiffly told him. 'I'm not thirsty.'

'Well,' he looked doubtful, 'we'll be a couple of hours. It's a long wait.'

'That's OK. It's what I'm being paid for, after all.'

Sebastian didn't grace her curt statement with a response.

Instead, he climbed out and slammed the door behind him.

She watched them walk through the entrance to the hotel. Despite her irritation with him, she felt childish. But really, did he think she had money to burn? She snorted to herself. I mean she could just imagine the price of a coffee in a place like this.

A tap on her side window startled her. It was Sebastian again. She pressed the button that electronically operated the window. 'Yes?'

'I should have said. You'll get your expenses reimbursed for anything you spend while in our employ. Just get a receipt,' and he was gone once more.

Huh! Did he think she was so hard up she couldn't afford a cup of coffee? she wondered, completely disregarding the fact that that's exactly what she'd been thinking just seconds ago.

OK then, she'd do as he said. She could use a coffee, in actual fact. The drive here had been a stressful one, taking into account that it wasn't her car, and that if she did have a bump it would probably cost several thousands of pounds to repair. Not that Sebastian wouldn't have insurance, but still.

She strode into the cafe, ignoring the amused glances at her casual top and trousers, everyone inside was dressed as if going to a fashion show, and found an empty table. An equally smartly dressed waitress took her order for a cappuccino and a toasted tea cake.

'I'm sorry, Madam, we don't do toasted tea cakes,' the woman told her, looking down her long nose as she did so.

'A pastry then.'

'Thank you, Madam.'

Good grief, thought Erin, didn't the rich every fancy a warm, butter-laden tea cake? Mind you, she couldn't for the life of her imagine Sebastian tucking into a tea cake, melting butter dripping off his chin. She chuckled at the image. Pity, really. It would render him fractionally more human.

Once she was back in the car, she pulled out the handbook and made a thorough study of it, familiarising herself with all of the vehicle's features. It had every luxury she could think of and a few she couldn't. She was still deeply engrossed when Sebastian and Valerie returned.

'Glad to see you learning the tricks of your trade,' was Sebastian's opening remark.

9

The journey back to Willow Green and
Sebastian's home passed uneventfully,
so effortless was the powerful car to
drive. It also passed without Erin
gleaning a single fact with which to help
her and her mother in their struggle.
The man possessed all the qualities of a
clam, she decided. Not a single mention
was made of his plans.

Once they were back, Erin retired to
the small room that they labelled *Erin's
office*. Sebastian had given her a sheet
of notes to put into some sort of order.
They were details of the meeting. To
Erin's disappointment, they had nothing to do with the new leisure centre.
Which, when she considered it, wasn't
surprising. He'd hardly feed her with
the ammunition she needed.

It was two days later that Sebastian
came to Erin's office and said, 'I need

to go to Cornwall tomorrow for a meeting. I'd like you to accompany me.'

'Me?' Erin stared at him in dismay.

'Yes.' His gaze was perfectly level as it met hers. 'Is that a problem?'

'We-ell, um . . . why do you need me? To drive?'

'Maybe. I need you there to take notes for me. It's a preliminary meeting to discuss the building of a leisure complex.'

'Another?' she queried drily.

'Yes. And I need a written record of everything that's said.'

'But surely you must employ a secretary, a PA?'

'I do, but I wish you to come.'

'I'll have to ask your sister, I was originally employed by her, after all.'

'I've done that. She's OK about it. So, can you be here for seven o'clock tomorrow morning? It's a good four hour drive to Penzance.'

'Four hours. Each way?' She was horror struck.

'Uh-huh. We'll share the driving.'

And that was how Erin found herself driving down the M5 the next morning, Sebastian at her side, studying papers — just as he'd done on the way to Birmingham.

By eleven-thirty, they were pulling up outside a large hotel on the outskirts of Penzance.

'Good,' Sebastian said, the first time he'd spoken in about two-and-a-half hours. He'd remained engrossed in whatever the documents were that he'd brought with him. 'You made excellent time. Not too tired, I hope. I'll drive back later so you'll be able to relax. Right. You have a notebook and pen?'

Erin nodded.

'Good. So into the fray,' and he gestured for her to enter the hotel ahead of him.

Five-and-a-half hours later, they walked out, to find themselves peering through driving rain. It was so severe, it splashed several inches off the tarmac in front of them.

'Oh no,' Sebastian muttered. 'That

settles it. I'm not driving back in this.'

There was a strangely satisfied expression upon his face, Erin saw. Why on earth should he be pleased that it was pouring with rain? Just so that she would drive and not him? Her shoulders sagged. She was bone weary. She'd driven for four-and-a-half hours, taken notes all day. Even her fingers ached.

But that clearly wasn't what Sebastian meant at all because he headed back inside, straight for the receptionist's desk, and asked, 'Would it be possible to have two rooms for the night?'

'Certainly, Sir. That's no problem,' the smiling girl answered him. She wasn't quite batting her long, black eyelashes, Erin saw with irritation.

'Um . . . ' Erin hastened over to him, 'we can't stay the night.'

He glanced back at her. 'Why not?'

'Because I'm expected back, that's why.'

He thrust a hand into his jacket pocket and brought out a mobile phone. 'Here, ring whoever's expecting you. I'm sure he'll wait.' His smile was full of irony.

She didn't take it. 'I have my own, thank you, and it's not a he.'

'Oh, is it not?'

'No.'

He was clearly waiting for her to tell him who it was. Erin held her silence. It was none of his business. But apart from that, how would it sound if she said the person waiting was her mother? Knowing him, he'd probably laugh out loud and make some sarcastic remark about little girls needing Mummy's permission to stay out for the night. She wouldn't give him the satisfaction.

'Anyway, we have no clothes with us.'

He pointed towards several small boutiques to one side of the foyer. 'Buy something, the company will pay.'

And that was that.

Once she was in her room, she phoned Jill. Jill was surprised but not concerned. 'I'll see you tomorrow then. I've got to go, darling, I'm going out.'

Erin turned off her phone, her

expression thoughtful. What was Jill up to? She'd never known her go out so often in the evenings.

She'd done as Sebastian had suggested and bought necessities. She'd drawn the line at anything else. Luckily, she'd dressed smartly for the day in a lightweight suit and blouse.

True, it was creased, but nothing a steam in the bathroom wouldn't remove.

She'd hoped to order some food from Room Service and eat alone, but Sebastian had other ideas.

'I'll see you in the bar in an hour or so, we'll have a drink and then go into dinner.'

Meekly, she'd agreed, but now, lying back in the scented water of a hot bath, her stomach began to churn. The last person she wanted to spend the evening with was Sebastian Rivers.

But once they were seated at the dinner table, Sebastian proved himself very good company. He told her about himself, he was self-made, with fingers in many pies: the engineering industry, catering; he supplied ready prepared food to hotels and schools. He was involved in the private housing development market, and had constructed several large shopping complexes.

'I've only just moved into the leisure business. In fact, Willow Green is the first.'

'Providing it's built, of course,' Erin smartly put in.

'Naturally.' His gaze met hers easily. 'But it will be a steep learning curve.'

'Tell me, don't you ever feel remorse at having to put people out of their homes?'

'In some cases, yes.' His fingers curled around the stem of his wine glass, his dark gaze holding hers, unrepentant, resolute. 'When it's people like your mother who really don't want to move. But they're always offered very generous compensation and, to be honest, the majority of people jump at it.'

'Unlike my mother.'

'Unlike your mother.' His mouth quirked at the corners. 'Tell you what.

Why don't we call a truce for tonight? Put business aside. Tell me about yourself.'

So she did, although she was sorely tempted to ask him why he'd looked so pleased at their having to stay overnight. Could this have been his aim all along? Was that why he'd insisted she accompany him? Had he hoped to get her on her own, away from other influences, and persuade her to persuade her mother to move out. Although how could he have known it would rain so hard? Not even he could have anticipated that, surely?

The meal they were served was excellent, as were the wines, and when they'd had their fill of both, Erin to the extent of feeling decidedly tipsy, Sebastian suggested they call it a day.

'It's been a tiring few hours.'

'Come on.' He held out a hand. 'Let's go. I'll take you back to your room and then leave you.' Warm amusement gleamed at her.

Erin couldn't help herself. She took

his hand. It felt so right; so good. She sighed as they walked into the lift.

'OK?' he asked.

He'd clearly heard her sigh.

'Oh yes,' she murmured. 'I'm OK. In fact, I'm very OK.' She leant against the back wall of the lift and closed her eyes. Her head spun, so she opened them again pretty smartly. Sebastian was standing very close. So close his face was blurred.

'Erin.'

Erin's breath caught in her throat. He was going to kiss her. She wanted him to kiss her, to see if it was as exciting as it had been before. She closed her eyes again, tilting her head towards him.

'Erin.'

'Yes.' Dreamily, she opened her eyes.

'It's our floor.'

'Oh.' To her dismay, disappointment raged within her. Silently, she followed him as, with a hand at her elbow, he guided her to her bedroom door.

'Have you got your key?'

'Yes, somewhere.' Her head spun as

she rummaged in her bag. She really shouldn't have drunk so much wine. That could be the only excuse for the way her emotions were rampaging. 'Here it is.'

He took it from her and opened the door. 'There you are then.'

She stared up at him. Wasn't he going to kiss her?

'Goodnight, I'll see you in the morning.'

His expression was a strange one now, she saw. A mixture of amusement and yes, regret. Despite that, though, he left her and walked to his own door.

He didn't turn, not even once.

10

Erin awoke with a start — and a raging headache. She groaned, burying her head beneath the pillow. Why had she drunk so much? It had been stupid! She groaned again. Oh no. That was by no means the worst of it. Memories of the final moments of the evening before were starting to surface.

No, no. She shook the pillow off. Whatever must Sebastian have thought?

It took a long, cold shower to clear her head, but it ensured that she felt marginally more composed by the time she left her room.

Fortunately, Sebastian appeared to have erased any memory of the evening before. Huh! He was probably used to women throwing themselves at him. Just look at how the receptionist had reacted to him. So — what would one more be?

As he'd promised, he took the wheel for the long journey back and conversation was minimal. He evidently preferred to concentrate on the road. Erin didn't mind. She didn't feel like talking either.

Once back in her office, she worked until five, as she and Valerie had initially agreed she would, and then just as she'd always done throughout her working life, she tidied her desk. She was on her way across the hallway when she heard Sebastian in his office.

'Harry, you all set for tonight?' There was a pause, then, 'Let's hope it goes well. If it does, it should settle matters one way or another, I should think.' Erin could hear the smile in his voice.

Unable to resist the temptation to hear more, she crept closer to the door. If she could learn precisely what was planned for tonight? Eavesdropping wasn't something she would normally think of indulging in, but this was an exception.

'Aah, just off.'

Erin practically leapt out of her skin. It was Valerie.

'Um, yes. There's nothing else you want me to do, is there?'

My Lord! Supposing she'd turned up while Erin had had her ear pressed to Sebastian's office door? How embarrassing would that have been? As it was, she was clearly wondering why Erin was creeping across the hall.

'No. I'll see you tomorrow.' She gave Erin a very strange look. 'Did you wish to see Sebastian?'

'Heaven's, no.' Erin gave a light laugh.

She got home to find Jill yet again preparing to go out.

'Ah, there you are. I'm off to Nina's.'

Erin regarded her. 'You look very nice. Off somewhere posh again?'

'No, um, well, maybe, I'm not sure. Must go, darling. I'll see you later.'

'Well, you might not. I think I'll go and see Sophie. I don't feel like spending the evening alone.' She'd better ring her friend first though, make sure she was going to be in. There was no point in walking over there if she wasn't.

Sophie was going to be in. 'Hair

washing night,' she told Erin. 'You can give me a hand. You always did do a mean blow dry.'

By the time Erin had had something to eat and left to go to her friend's house, it was raining heavily. She peered through the downpour. Maybe she should drive? But there was invariably a problem parking in that road. The houses didn't have driveways. She shrugged on an old raincoat of her mother's. A drop of rain wouldn't hurt her.

How wrong could she have been? The rain didn't hurt her, but it very swiftly soaked through the old mac and within minutes she was bitterly regretting her decision to walk. She trudged on, however, having judged that it would take her as long to go back for her car as it would to continue, and she'd soon dry out at Sophie's. She was picking her way round a particularly deep puddle when she spotted another person doing the same thing further along the road. It was Nina, Jill's friend.

Of Jill, there was no sign.

'Nina,' Erin called, 'is Mum . . . '

But Nina had already scurried away, and scurry was the right word. It was as if the other woman had seen Erin and then gone to some lengths to avoid having to stop and speak.

Strange! Erin wrinkled her brow. Nina was usually the friendliest of souls. Maybe she hadn't recognised Erin through the rain. It was the only explanation that Erin could come up with.

Erin stood on the kerbside, still pondering the other woman's peculiar behaviour and preparing herself to dodge the traffic to get across to Sophie's, when a low slung sports car accelerated past her, straight through a large puddle, dispatching the better part of the contents straight up at Erin. The water hit her full on.

'Aah,' she gasped. 'Idiot!' she shouted from beneath her dripping umbrella, only to belatedly realise who it was in the car.

Sebastian — with a woman. The woman whose car it was clearly as she was the one driving.

'Oh good grief!' If she'd been wet before, she was positively drenched now. The water literally ran off her mac, down over her legs and into her shoes.

They couldn't have noticed what they'd done, or surely they would have stopped, offered some sort of apology, wouldn't they? Erin bent down and mopped her legs as best as she could with a tissue.

Nonetheless, she couldn't stop herself from wondering who the woman had been? She hadn't looked very old, eighteen, or maybe nineteen. And she hadn't been local, Erin would have recognised her. Her anger intensified mingled with something else — Jealousy? Whatever is was, it was sharp and painful.

It was some three hours later that she returned home. Thankfully, the rain had stopped and the stars were twinkling. As she walked through the night she heard a burglar alarm ring. At first, she thought nothing of it. It was only as she got nearer the shop that she realised that that was where it was coming from.

Dreading what she was going to find, she broke into a run. Sure enough, the shop window had been smashed, the brick that had been used still lying in the midst of the broken glass.

Erin was puzzled. A quick glance revealed that nothing had been taken, some stock had been damaged that was all, which suggested that the culprit had been merely trying to intimidate again rather than steal. She let herself into the shop and immediately rang the police. Then she turned the burglar alarm off.

It was as she was doing that that she recalled the conversation that she'd overheard that afternoon between Sebastian and Harry. What was it Sebastian had said? 'You all set for tonight? Let's hope it goes well. If it does, it should settle matters.' Was this what he'd been referring to? Were he and Harry trying to frighten Jill into agreeing to move?

Declan was the first person on the scene after Erin.

'I saw the broken window. What happened?'

Erin pointed to the brick. 'Someone obviously lobbed that through the glass.'

'You weren't here, were you?' he quietly asked. 'Or your mum?'

'No. I'd gone to Sophie's and Mum's with a — a friend.' Which friend she was no longer so sure about after seeing Nina alone. Although to be fair, maybe Jill had been waiting at Nina's house? But if that were the case, why hadn't Nina stopped when Erin hailed her? 'Maybe if we'd been here it wouldn't have happened.'

Declan stared around. 'What's been taken?'

'Nothing as far as I can see.'

'Nothing?'

'Well, it's obvious, isn't it? It's more intimidation. Whoever it was didn't want anything other than to scare my mother and I out of the place. Either that, or I interrupted them before they could grab anything.'

'No, it sounds as if you're spot on. It's more intimidation. Look, I really think it might be better to concede defeat and move out before someone's hurt.'

Tears stung Erin's eyes. She gave a tiny sob.

'Oh, love, come here,' and he pulled her into his arms. 'I'm right, you know. You've put up a good fight, but it's time to call it quits.'

'I can't believe that Sebastian would do something like this.'

'Well, who else could it be?' He rocked her back and forth, dropping small kisses on to her head. 'I mean, think about it.'

She was and wondering whether she should tell him about the conversation she'd overheard this afternoon at Sebastian's? Share her suspicions of his father's involvement? He might not take too kindly to hearing her accuse Harry. She needed proof first.

'Oh, Erin, I wish you'd let me take care of you. We could get a place together. Your mum could take the compensation and move.'

'Well, well, what a tender little scene.'

They sprang apart. Sebastian Rivers stood there, dark eyes blazing. 'I saw the window in passing.'

Erin simply couldn't help herself. 'My word,' she retorted, 'what a lot of people just happen to be passing.'

Declan wasn't so polite. 'This is down to you, Rivers, isn't it?'

'Don't be more ridiculous than you already are, Stubbs. Why would I do something like this?' Sebastian's gaze had all the properties of polished steel.

'To scare us,' Erin bluntly said.

'Yeah, you want the place vacated, don't you?' Declan put in. 'Well, it looks like you've won.'

'Declan,' Erin gasped, 'I haven't agreed to that.'

But Sebastian didn't appear to have heard Declan's impulsive words. He was staring intently at Erin. 'You really think I'd do something like this? To scare you?' He paused, regarding her reflectively. 'Were you here when it happened?'

'No, fortunately I'd gone to visit a friend.' She didn't mention that she'd seen him on her way, with a girl. Which, now she came to think of it, made it strange that he should be here now. Her glance darted beyond him, he was in his own car. She decided to find out why.

'I saw you earlier in a sports car,' she said. 'In fact, you went through a puddle and thoroughly drenched me.'

'Oh, that would have been Suzy. The daughter of a friend of mine. Sorry, we didn't see you.'

'So,' she made a point of glancing at his vehicle, 'how come you're in yours now?'

His face hardened. 'I left it at my friend's house, he's in hospital, we were going to visit him. It seemed easier to go in the same car and . . . ' he stopped as if wondering why he was bothering to explain all this to her, 'I'm on my way home. Any more questions?'

'No.' She could hardly go on quizzing him on the coincidence of his arrival right after a break in. Not now that she worked for him. She gave a silent groan. Instead of aiding her fight against him, her involvement with him was actually working against her.

He turned back to Declan. 'Just as a matter of interest, where were you, Stubbs, while this was going on? I presume it's only just happened.'

'That's right, and where I was is none of your business.'

'I beg to disagree. If you're insinuating that it's intimidation, then it's as much to your benefit as mine to scare Erin and her mother away. I'm sure you'll have a share in whatever Harry stands to make from the deal. So, I ask you again. Where were you?'

Declan was looking edgy, shifty, even. 'I was with a friend.'

'I see. And your friend will verify that?'

'Yes.' He flicked a glance at Erin. 'I

was with Laura.'

'Laura!' Erin cried.

'Yes. And I don't want you to read anything into that, Erin. We had things to talk about.'

Erin understood his expression of uncertainty now. Guilt, even? She shrugged. 'It's really none of my business who you see, Declan. You're a free agent.'

Her complete lack of emotion about this told her more clearly than anything that she had no feelings of any sort, other than friendship that is, for Declan.

Whereas when she'd spotted Sebastian with his young companion, well, that had been very different.

The breath snagged in her throat as she recalled her overwhelming desire for him to kiss her at the hotel. She couldn't be falling for him — could she?

'It is your business, Erin,' Declan insisted, 'I care about you.'

Sebastian gave a snort of contempt at

that. 'Really. So you go off and meet another woman to prove that? Really, Stubbs.'

Declan whirled, and bringing up a fist, punched Sebastian.

Or, at least, he would have if Sebastian hadn't sidestepped out of the way.

'You!' Declan growled, 'Keep your nose out of this.'

Sebastian brushed him aside as if he were no more than a troublesome fly. 'I take it you've called the police?' he asked Erin.

'Yes. They should be here shortly.'

'I'll wait then.'

'There's no need. I'll be fine.'

'I'll be the judge of that.'

'If he's staying, then so will I.' Declan said, clearly determined not to be outdone in the gallantry stakes.

Erin sighed. Not for the first time, she was feeling like a rag doll, being pulled this way and that.

Luckily, two police constables turned up at that point.

They listened to what Erin had to say, but swiftly lost interest once she told them that nothing had been taken.

'Bit strange that,' one of them remarked.

'Not if all you wanted was to frighten someone,' Declan said.

'Maybe you'd care to explain that statement, Sir,' the police officer said.

'Certainly.' Which he then proceeded to do, firmly pointing the finger of suspicion at Sebastian.

'And who's to say it wasn't you, Stubbs? You must have been pretty near to show up so promptly, date with the lovely Laura or not.'

'Gentlemen, please,' the officer wearily said, 'if you'd both like to make a statement detailing where you were and till what time.'

Once the statements were duly noted, the two policemen left. Nobody took much notice of their promise to look into things. 'But with nothing actually taken . . . ' one of them had said with a shrug.

It wasn't long after this that Jill turned up. Erin had finally managed to persuade both men to go. She'd wanted nothing more than to be left in peace, primarily to examine the feelings which she'd uncovered that night. To try and decide if they really were what they seemed.

'My goodness!' Jill rushed, pointing at the broken window, against which Erin, with the help of both Sebastian and Declan, had fixed a large piece of plywood in order to provide some protection from the elements until morning, 'What happened?'

Erin told her.

'Oh no. The insurance company will want me to install all sorts of alarm devices now and, frankly, I can't afford it. Business just isn't good enough any more.'

It was true that the local people had all but withdrawn their custom. Their way of making their feelings known over Jill's continuing refusal to move, Erin guessed.

'I'm a bit more concerned over whoever it is that is doing this,' Erin told her.

Again, she couldn't decide whether to tell her mother what she'd overheard earlier. She had no evidence to prove that Sebastian and Harry had been discussing a break in. And it could just worry Jill even more. She decided, for the second time that evening, to keep her suspicions to herself. Even so, she was surprised to hear Jill stoutly defend Harry.

'Well, it definitely wasn't Harry.'

'How on earth do you know that? I mean, it's very important to him that we leave. Just as important as it is to Sebastian. More so, possibly. I mean, Sebastian's a very wealthy man, you only have to look at his house to know that — and I know he's got several other projects under way.

'This particular one going wrong would hardly bankrupt him. Whereas Harry badly needs the money that Sebastian will pay him.'

'Erin, Harry wouldn't,' Jill continued to insist, 'he simply wouldn't. I've known him for years and it just isn't his style. Anyway, how do we know it isn't one of my ex-customers venting their wrath over my refusal to move out? Have you considered that? You're far too ready in my opinion to blame Harry.'

Erin had no answer to that question. And she supposed that Jill could be right. It would let Sebastian off the hook if she was. What a relief that would be. She chose not to probe too deeply into why it would be such a relief. She wasn't quite ready yet to face up to the full implications of her growing feelings for Sebastian Rivers.

Even so, her suspicions were still powerful enough to keep her awake for the better part of the night. The main thing worrying her was that it had been an almighty coincidence Sebastian turning up like that earlier. If it had been him behind it, could he have been waiting just round the corner to see how she'd react to the brick going through the window? It was a very strong possibility.

Maybe he'd hoped that it would prove the final straw and she'd throw herself upon him, saying, 'OK, I give up.' That's certainly what Declan had assumed she'd do.

No, no matter what it looked like, she simply couldn't see Sebastian doing something like that. But if it wasn't him, who had it been?

It was then that she realised that in the stress of it all she'd quite forgotten to ask Jill where she'd been when she'd seen Nina — alone.

11

The following morning, Erin was tired and on edge and sorely tempted not to show up at work. She and Declan had practically accused Sebastian of being behind the break in. Well, Declan had actually done the accusing, but she'd said nothing to demonstrate that she disagreed. In fact, she'd supplied the reasons why he could have been the one responsible. He could well refuse to let her into the house.

She groaned, eyeing the broken window. What a mess. How could she be attracted to a man whom she suspected of terrorising two women? What kind of human being was she?

Her feelings of self-disgust intensified when Harry arrived at the Rivers' residence. She heard Valerie saying, 'Sebastian, Harry's here.'

'Oh good. Show him in, please.'

Erin pricked up her ears and moved towards her own open door. If only she could hear what they were about to say? It could be the proof that they were behind last night's break in. Maybe if she heard Sebastian admit to the intimidation, her feelings for him would wither and die? But then again, if the meeting was about something else entirely, well — she could maybe feel free to love?

All her efforts came to nought, however. For Harry firmly closed the door behind him and try as she might, apart from the low rumble of their voices, she couldn't hear a single word.

That evening, Jill once again went out. Not quite as finely dressed as the evening before but still in a very smart outfit.

'Nina again?' Erin drily asked. For some reason, she couldn't bring herself to quiz Jill about where she was going, to all but accuse her of lying. But she was almost sure it wasn't Nina that Jill was going to meet.

'Mmm,' Jill absently answered. She headed for the door, clearly keen to be gone.

Really! What was wrong with everyone? They were all hiding something.

Erin finished straightening the magazines and then, with no sign of any more customers, decided to shut the shop early for once. Normally, they remained open until eight o'clock or thereabouts, which was why Erin had taken over once she'd returned from Kinnerton.

Since she'd been home, she'd fallen into the habit of doing the last couple of hours of the day, in order to give her mother a break — unless she herself was going out, of course.

She was preparing a sandwich and resigning herself to a solitary evening in when the bell on the side door which led directly up a flight of stairs to the flat rang. She glanced out of the window and saw Declan standing there. She buzzed him in and listened as he climbed the stairs, two at a time by the sound of it.

'Hi,' he greeted her as he strode in. 'I

wondered if you wanted to go out somewhere? Take your mind off the happenings of last night.'

Erin had decided that it wasn't fair to let him go on hoping that there could be something between them, something more than friendship, and here was her opportunity. It was going to hurt him, she knew that, but it had to be done.

'I don't think so, Declan.'

'Aw, come on. A drink? I could even run to a meal.'

'No, Declan.' Her heart was beating fit to burst from her chest. She hated having to hurt anyone, especially someone like Declan, whom she'd known for many years and to whom she'd once been so close. It had to be said though, and the sooner the better. 'Look, there's something you should know.'

How well did she really know Declan? she belatedly wondered. She had no idea of how he would take her rejection. Angrily? Sadly?

'Um, I don't feel what you feel.'

'Huh? What're you on about?'

'Declan, please listen.'

He was starting to look confused now. He shook his head. 'I don't follow.'

'Well,' Erin searched for the least hurtful words. 'You're fond of me, yes?'

His look of confusion had changed to one of apprehension. 'More than fond, actually.'

'Precisely. That's not how I feel about you.' There, she'd said it.

Declan's eyes never left her. 'Go on.'

'Well,' she spread her hands, 'that's it. I don't feel anything more than friendship, And I don't think I ever will.'

'You can't know that.'

'I do. I'm sorry; very sorry.'

He looked like a small boy who was being denied the toy that he wanted.

He pulled her towards him. Erin jerked away from him. 'No, Declan — listen to me.'

'I've listened to you long enough.' And he grabbed her again, pressing his mouth to hers.

For the first time then, she felt real fear.

The doorbell rang. Declan lifted his head. 'Who the blazes is that?'

Making the most of his momentary distraction, Erin wrenched herself free. 'I'll go see,' she gasped.

'Blast you,' Declan suddenly shouted. 'I gave Laura up for you.'

'I'm sorry, but I didn't ask you to.'

'I'll never forgive you for this.'

Declan strode out of the flat, down the stairs to yank the door open.

Erin had followed him down and, to her horror, saw Sebastian standing there.

She hadn't seen him all day, which had come as something of a relief, it had to be said. She'd glimpsed him leaving the house with Harry after their meeting and he hadn't returned.

'You're OK. I'm just leaving,' Declan snorted. He glanced back at Erin. His eyes contained a look of utter contempt.

'Erin,' Sebastian looked at her as well now. There was no sign of anger, or condemnation on his face. Instead, all she could see was concern. 'Are you all right?'

'I'm fine. Declan . . . '

But Declan had pushed past Sebastian and was on his way down the road. He walked fast and was quickly out of sight, and out of her life too?

'Erin?'

She blinked at Sebastian.

'Are you OK? You look shaken. Upset.' He too gazed in the direction in which Declan had gone. 'Did he do anything?' His gaze darkened as it came to rest upon her once more. She could see him absorbing the signs of disarray: her tousled hair, her shadowed eyes.

Her face paled and she began to shake even harder than she had been.

She entered the flat. He did the same; he was close enough that she could feel his breath on the back of her neck. He reached out and turned her to face him.

'You need a drink,' Sebastian said. 'A brandy.' He glanced at her questioningly.

This wasn't going at all as she'd expected. She'd expected to be subjected to an inquisition, harangued — threatened, even. Instead, here he was, taking care of her.

Erin sipped tentatively at the amber liquid, shuddering and pulling a face as she did so. She never drank spirits, wine — yes, but even that she tried not to overdo.

However, eventually — and with much urging from Sebastian — she did drink it. She held out the empty glass. Sebastian took it from her and placed it on the table.

'So — are you going to tell me what happened?'

'I can't — sorry.' She could only manage the weakest of smiles, as much as she wanted to breezily laugh everything off. Mainly because her mouth would only tremble.

He moved fractionally closer. 'Come here then.'

Meekly, she did as she was told. Her resolve seemed to have totally disappeared. Sebastian slid both arms about her. He smiled down at her.

The first thing she knew of his intention was the feel of his mouth on hers, so lightly, so impossibly tenderly, so different to how Declan's kiss had felt.

She felt utterly, utterly safe.

'Erin,' he murmured throatily.

'No.' Erin's eyes were open, in every sense of the word. It was as if she were dragging herself out of a drugged sleep. She wrenched herself away from him. 'No, I — we can't do this, it's wrong.'

Then she opened her eyes and stared at him. His expression was the bleakest she'd ever seen on anyone. Declan's hurt a moment ago hadn't come anywhere near. A cold voice asked, 'Wrong? Why?'

'Why?' she cried. 'Because we're on opposite sides. You stand for everything that I . . . ' She stopped.

'Well,' his voice was harsh, cruel, 'go on, say it.'

'Hate,' she whispered. 'We're fighting each other, for heaven's sake.'

'So are your mother and Harry,' he'd obviously decided to disregard the word *hate*. Erin drew a breath of relief. 'But it hasn't stopped them.'

Erin stared. 'Stopped them? What do you mean?' Her heart had almost stopped beating, as if in sympathy with the words.

'Falling in love.'

'What on earth are you talking about?' But she knew. So that's what had been going on. Her mother and Harry. Having secret meetings, dates. Why hadn't she guessed? So did that mean . . . ? Her heart missed several beats. Did that mean that it was Sebastian, on his own, who'd been responsible? Or was it someone else entirely?

Sebastian gave an ironic grin. 'Aah, I see you understand.'

'But how?'

He threw back his head and snorted with laughter. 'Don't be naive, Erin. How do you think? They've been meeting, going out.'

A single, terrible question framed

itself then within Erin's head. Had Harry courted Jill simply to try and get her agreement to move out of the flat and the shop? Would he be that calculating? That merciless? And what about when he'd got his way, would he then just drop her?

'Was this your idea?' she spat.

'Oh Lord! Here we go.' Sebastian sounded unutterably weary rather than angry with her. 'Why should it have been my idea? What's it to do with me? Why do you always blame me for everything?'

'Well, what do you expect? You're the obvious culprit. You and Harry are desperate for her to leave. So is that it? He's seduced her to get her agreement?'

'I don't believe you,' he bit the words out. 'Do you think so little of your mother that you believe she's unworthy of a good man's love without there being some, some ulterior motive? They're in love, Erin, genuinely in love. He's felt that way for a couple of years now. So I suggest you talk to Jill about it. Maybe she can convince you it's all above board. Especially when she tells you he asked her to marry him. Does that sound as if he's merely trying to seduce her?'

'Oh, I'll talk to her, don't you worry. Anyway, all that aside, why exactly did you come here tonight?'

He seemed surprised at her sudden firing of that question. 'Ah, yes. I'm here to tell you what I've decided.'

'Oh really. What you've decided.' She spoke sarcastically. 'So what's that then? That you'd decided to seduce me into agreement as well?'

His cold tones continued, relentlessly. 'I came to tell you that I've changed my mind. I'm going to scale down my plans for the leisure centre. It doesn't have to be that big. In fact, smaller could mean more luxurious. And the woodland will be left untouched.

'I've already told Harry, so you see, there's no reason for him to seduce your mother into any sort of agreement

— other than to agree to marry him, of course. The shop will be left standing so she can go on running that, if she should choose to. You could even go on living in the flat, if you wished to.'

Erin closed her eyes. That's probably what they'd been talking about this morning. And possibly when she'd overheard Sebastian on the phone yesterday, Harry had been confiding his plans, his hopes concerning Jill, to Sebastian? It all made sense. What had she done? She'd have to apologise immediately.

'Sebastian . . . ' But when she opened her eyes again, it was to find herself alone.

12

By the time her mother arrived home, Erin felt much the worse for wear. 'Erin?' Jill anxiously asked. 'Are you all right, darling?' She regarded the empty glass quizzically. 'Have you been drinking?' She lifted the glass and sniffed at it. 'Brandy! What on earth's happening?'

'I had some news tonight,' Erin woozily said.

'Have you? What?' Jill regarded her daughter uncertainly.

'You — you and Harry. What's been going on?'

A tinge of pink coloured Jill's cheek. 'Aah. Who told you?'

'Sebastian Rivers was here,' Erin told her. 'He said Harry's proposed.'

'I see.'

'Have you accepted him?'

'Yes.'

'But — but why didn't you tell me? Why all the lies? The sneaking around? Using Nina as your alibi?'

'I'm sorry about that, but I wasn't sure how you'd take it.' Jill looked at her sheepishly. 'I've been trying to pluck up the courage.'

'Are you in love with him?'

'Oh yes. Very much.'

'I see. So . . . '

'Erin,' Jill interrupted, 'Sebastian has said he'll scale down his plans, but I'm moving out. Obviously I'll live with Harry. So I'm going to tell him to go ahead with his original plan. It's what everyone wants. Is that all right with you?'

'Fine. And, after all, Harry does need the money,' Erin bluntly declared.

'Well, Sebastian had agreed to still pay him a very substantial sum, so it's not just the money. I've had time to think about it all and it would be good for the village. The only thing is, where will you live?'

'Don't worry about me. I won't be

here. I only returned and then stayed for you in the first place. I'll go back to Birmingham. I would like to know who was behind all the trouble, though.'

Jill shrugged. 'Some of the local people I should think. It definitely wasn't Harry or Sebastian, I'd stake my life on that.'

Something suddenly occurred to Erin and she started to giggle. 'Oh, my Lord! All this means that Declan and I will be step-brother and sister. I wonder how he'll feel about that?'

Sadly, Erin's amusement wasn't destined to last. Her aching head the next morning saw to that. That wasn't the worst of it, however. The worst of it was what she recalled saying to Sebastian.

She groaned. She'd accused him of wanting to seduce her in order to get his own way over the new centre. How on earth could she go on working for him?

She couldn't. She did the only thing she could. She rang Valerie and told her she was ill, too ill to go to work.

'You will be back, though, won't you?' Valerie anxiously asked. 'You've been so much help to Sebastian and I.'

Huh! thought Erin. She wasn't sure that Sebastian would agree with that sentiment any longer. He'd most likely be glad to be shot of her.

'I'm not sure. I really ought to get back to Birmingham. I've got a flat there standing empty.'

'Oh, I see.' And that was that.

She hung around the shop and the flat, depressed and unhappy until even Jill, in the end, snapped at her. 'For heaven's sake, pull yourself together. Go and see Sebastian. Apologise.'

For she'd told her mother, naturally, what had happened between them, the awful things she'd said.

Harry put in a shame-faced appearance later that day, apparently intent on speaking to Erin. 'Your mother will have told you what's going on, no doubt.'

'She has,' Erin replied. Her anger at their secrecy had vanished. They were so obviously in love. 'Congratulations. When is the wedding to be?'

'Oh, all in good time.' He smiled complacently. 'We want to do things right. Nothing is to be rushed.'

'I see.' Erin hid a smile. 'So you'll both be living at the farm?'

'Oh yes.' He gave Erin a sharp look then. She wondered whether Sebastian had told him of the things she'd said? Of Erin's deep suspicions of his motives for proposing marriage? She hoped not. She didn't want to put a damper on the couple's happiness.

'I just wanted you to know, Erin, I've loved your mother for quite some time now, but she didn't feel the same — not till recently, that is.' He beamed lovingly at Jill. 'Anyway, you need have no worries. I'll do all I can to make her happy.' His smile disappeared. 'Now, I'm not just here to talk about all that. I'm here to confess.'

Erin tensed. He wasn't about to confess to the vandalism, was he?

'It was Declan. He was the one

responsible for all your troubles.'

Erin gaped at him, as did Jill.

'Declan? Why for heaven's sake?' she demanded to know. 'He assured me he wasn't concerned over it all. Why, he backed me in front of Sebastian.'

'I know. But he thought he was doing me a favour; helping me out,' Harry said. 'He knew how much I needed the money from the sale.'

'Oh, Harry,' Jill cried. 'I'm so sorry.'

'You're sorry?' Erin exclaimed. 'Why?'

'Well, if I'd agreed to move in the first place, none of it would have been necessary. He was only thinking of his father.'

'Oh, Jill, my love.' Harry swept her into his arms. 'Only you could react to what I've just told you in so generous a fashion.' Love filled his eyes. Erin found her own gaze blurring too. If only she could find what they had. 'Anyway, he's coming round, in person. In fact,' he glanced towards the doorway, 'he's here now.'

And indeed he was.

Erin was speechless. Jill beckoned him in. 'Declan, come in, lad. Don't just stand there.'

'I'm so sorry, Mrs Kirkwood,' he said, 'and you, Erin. I can't tell you how much I regret it all. I can't think what possessed me.'

'And what about letting Sebastian take the blame?' Oh goodness, Erin accused him right up until last night. How differently things could have turned out if she hadn't suspected that he was the one behind it all.

'We accept your apology, Declan,' Jill said. 'There was no real damage done.'

'Erin?' Declan was pleading with her. 'I'm so sorry. Can you ever forgive me?'

What else could she say but, 'Yes.' He was about to be part of her family, after all. But she couldn't help thinking if only the situation between her and Sebastian could be resolved as easily.

But even that seemed destined to be sorted out, one way or the other.

Valerie turned up at the shop a week later. Erin still hadn't departed for her flat and a spot of job seeking. She'd rung Hal to see if her job was still there, but she was too late. He'd hired someone else.

So she really was out of work now. She'd well and truly burned her bridges, both with Hal and Sebastian.

'Erin,' Valerie said, 'I'm so relieved that you're still here.'

'Are you?'

'Yes.'

'I'm sorry, but I can't possibly come back to work for you. I'm sure your brother has told you.'

'Yes, he has.' Valerie's eyes twinkled momentarily. 'Do you realise what you've done to him? I've never seen him like this before. He's a man in torment.'

'Torment?' Erin didn't attempt to hide her confusion.

'Yes. He needs to see you.'

'Then why doesn't he?' she coolly asked. Well, as coolly as she could manage. Her heart was doing a strange little dance, and her pulse rate was threatening to go into overdrive.

'Because he thinks there's no chance . . .'

Erin wrinkled her brow. She was lost now. 'What? Of me coming back to work?'

'Why don't you go and see him? He'll tell you himself, I'm sure.'

'What? Right now?'

'That would be good. He is at home. Alone.' Valerie smiled encouragingly.

'We-ell, I don't know, we didn't exactly part on good terms.'

'Erin, that doesn't matter. Please.' Valerie's tone was one of heartfelt intensity. 'Please.'

Erin could hold out no longer. She had to know what her future held, whether the news be good or bad.

Seven minutes later precisely, she was parking outside of Sebastian's house. And it was at that point that she began to shake.

As she walked in through the open door — left open for her? she wondered.

If it was then Valerie must have

warned him she was on her way, because she saw him standing there, waiting, his expression saying it all. Her doubts vanished.

Slowly, very slowly, he held his arms out to her. She literally ran into them.

'I'm so sorry; so very sorry,' she said.

'Don't be,' he then murmured. 'I love you, Erin Kirkwood.'

THE END

AN UNEXPECTED ENCOUNTER

Fenella Miller

Miss Victoria Marsh has an un-expected encounter in the church with a handsome, but disagreeable, soldier who is recuperating from a grievous leg injury. Major Toby Highcliff believes himself to be a useless cripple, but meeting Victoria changes everything. Will he be able to keep her safe from the evil that stalks the neighbourhood and con-vince her he is the ideal man for her?

ANOTHER CHANCE

Rena George

School teacher Rowan Fairlie's life is set to change when Clett Drummond and his two young daughters take on the tenancy of Ballinbrae Farm. Clett insists he's come to the Highlands to help the girls recover from their mother's death, but Rowan suspects there's more to it. And why does her growing friendship with the family so infuriate the new laird, Simon Fraser? Is it simple jealousy — or are the two men linked by some terrible mystery from the past?

REBELLIOUS HEARTS

Susan Udy

Journalist Alice Jordan can't believe her misfortune when she literally bumps into entrepreneur Dominic Falconer. She is running a newspaper campaign to prevent him from destroying an ancient wood in his apparently never-ending pursuit of profit. However, when it becomes clear that local opinion is firmly on his side, Alice decides to go it alone. Someone has to stop him and she is more than ready for the battle. The trouble is — so is Dominic.

PASSAGE OF TIME

Janet Thomas

When charismatic Josh Stephens literally blows into her life, Melanie Treloar finds him a disturbing presence in the hostel she runs in west Cornwall. During his job of assessing some old mining remains Josh discovers a sea cave that holds an intriguing secret. When he is caught in a cliff fall — saving Melanie's niece — it is Melanie who comes to his rescue. Although this puts their relationship on a new level, can they solve the many problems that still remain?